North County Paranormal Unit

North County Paranormal Unit #1

Amanda McCormack

* 9 7 9 8 2 2 4 1 1 9 7 0 7 *

This one is dedicated to Andie Biagini. Thank you for a decade of writing together and here's to many more.

Contents

Want a Free Ebook?

CHAPTER 1

The house in question was a typical house in an ordinary suburban neighborhood in central Massachusetts. As she stood outside in the early summer sun, Gabriella double-checked the address on her phone, scrolling to the email she'd received from her cousin a few days earlier. This was it. This little raised ranch house that was set in among a neighborhood full of similar ranch houses. The vinyl siding was a grayish-blue and there was a small yard in front, with flowers lining a gravel walkway. A couple of cars were parked in the narrow driveway that led up to the garage. She could see that one of them had a cheerful stuffed rabbit in the back window.

A couple of cars drove past as she stood on the sidewalk beside her own car. The sound of them broke through the quiet morning air. This neighborhood seemed sleepy more than anything else, with only houses on the street and not a single business in sight. At least as far as she could see, that was. Further down, she could see a man mowing his front lawn, but that was the only other sign of life.

Gabriella slid her phone into her backpack and made her way up the walkway toward the house. It was nice enough, with a wide set of stairs leading up to the front door. More flowers spilled out of pots on each step, their scent seeming to bake out of them in the morning heat.

This looked cozy, like one of her many relatives' houses. Not like the headquarters of the best paranormal investigation team in the region. But the email her cousin James had sent her led straight here. So here went nothing.

She rang the doorbell and waited. After a few seconds, she heard footsteps from inside. The door opened and a young woman, maybe a little older than Gabriella, was standing there. "Bradley, your pizza is here!" she called back into the house. "Get your ass out here- oh."

She turned around and actually looked at Gabriella, her huge brown eyes wide. "Wait, you're not pizza."

Gabriella raised an eyebrow, then shook her head. "Not that I know of?"

The woman nodded, then her face lit up. "Oh! You're James's friend! Come on in!"

She pulled the door open further and gestured for Gabriella to follow her into the house. The front hallway did nothing to disperse the idea that this was a family home. The hall itself was tiny, with a short staircase leading down into the basement and up into the living room. Gabriella followed the woman up the carpeted blue stairs and up to the living room.

The living room was the first indicator that this house was anything out of the ordinary. Despite the cramped space in the room, three computers were scattered throughout it on several tables of varying sizes. Instead of family photos and mementos, the walls held a number of charts and bulletin boards. However, there were still two over-stuffed sofas sitting perpendicular to each other, separating the front hall from the living room somewhat.

Beyond the living room, Gabriella could see into the kitchen. It was cluttered and comfortable, with stacks of clean dishes and food containers scattered on the different surfaces. James stepped out from the kitchen and made his way over to them. He looked every inch the suburban dad with his broad shoulders, plaid shirt, and dirty-blond hair.

Despite the nine-year age gap between them, James and Gabriella had always been close. She hurried toward him.

"You came!" he exclaimed, wrapping her in a hug.

She gripped him tightly, feeling the familiar scratchiness of his worn flannel shirt. They held each other for a second and then, with a final squeeze, they let go. James grinned at her, then turned to the woman who'd let her in and was still standing there, watching curiously. "Amelia, this is my cousin Gabriella."

"Oh, you guys are cousins!" Amelia exclaimed. "I missed that somehow. Hey, nice to meet you!"

She gripped Gabriella's hand and gave it a firm shake. "He told me he had a fantastic candidate for the open position, but I didn't realize this stuff ran in the family."

James laughed. "You could say that, I guess."

Amelia nodded. "Great! Hey, I'll leave you to it."

She walked away, leaving them standing in the hallway. James smiled at Gabriella. "So how's your mom?"

"She's great," Gabriella replied. "Just finished her MBA, so she and her friend are on a celebratory cruise until next week."

"Oh yeah?" James asked with a smile. "Tell her congratulations for me. Does she know you're here?"

Apparently Gabriella hesitated just a little too long before answering. "I'm going to take that as a no?" James said, raising an eyebrow under his sandy hair.

Gabriella shrugged. "It's not that I'm avoiding telling her," she said. "I just...I don't need her permission, James. I'm twenty-two years old."

James held up his hands in surrender. "Hey, I'm not judging. But you should let her know at some point. At the very least so that we don't have to make up something plausible for Thanksgiving."

Gabriella grimaced, but didn't answer. James just moved on.

"So basically, the job is yours if you want it," he said. "My boss, Robin, gave me full permission and doesn't give a shit about family connections in the hiring process. I told him you were looking for a job and I thought you'd be a good addition to the team. So I have the all-clear to offer you the job."

"And this job is ghost hunting?"

James shrugged. "Kind of? That's part of it. But there are a whole lot more things going on that we need to deal with. Ghosts probably make up about fifty percent of what we do though, so your experience there will be helpful."

"My experience? James-"

"Like you didn't grow up in Gran's house?" James interrupted. "Gabs, you actually lived there, so you dealt with it plenty. You just grew up with it, so it's normal to you."

Gabriella didn't have a response to that. Not that she really wanted to argue anyway. She needed a job and her older cousin had called her up with an offer of one. Sure, it was chasing ghosts with him and his weird friends, but it paid and included health benefits.

"Is that what you do?" she asked. "Like, the stuff Gran did? With the salt and the cleansings?"

"Basically, yeah."

"And people pay you?"

"Uh, sometimes," James said, scratching his shoulder. "We didn't charge people for emergency services, there's enough funding coming from other sources. But sometimes we'll get hired in advance for less urgent work."

"And other people don't just do it themselves?"

She found that hard to believe. Even though she'd never actually done the cleansings herself, she'd always taken for granted that at least somebody in every family was in tune with the spirit world, whatever that even meant.

"Like I said," James said with a grin. "You grew up with it. You find it completely normal."

Gabriella shrugged. "That's fair."

Maybe this would be simple. She wasn't about to say that ghosts weren't real. But tossing some holy water around and telling ghosts to get out made people feel better whether there were really ghosts in their house or not. So while she'd always thought James's job was a little weird, it was no weirder than some of the other jobs in her family.

"So anyway, you have the job if you want it. We didn't drag you here for an interview. If you accept the job, today is basically the first orientation session. Do you want some coffee?"

"Sure."

James stepped into the kitchen and went over to the coffee machine sitting on the cluttered granite kitchen counter. He picked up a mug from the drying rack and poured a cup of coffee. "Anything in it?"

"Nah, black is good."

He handed her the coffee, and she took a sip. It was harsh and bitter, almost thick. Gabriella tried not to wince at the flavor. Normally she was just fine with black coffee, but this cup was a punishment.

"Come on," James said. "Let's go sit in the living room and we can talk for a little while. Then you can decide officially if you want the job or not."

Gabriella stopped with the coffee at her lips. What more was there for her to know? And what might potentially keep her from taking the job? Was there anything more surprising that might come up in a job interview for ghost hunting?

They stepped back out into the living room, where a man around James's age was standing at one of the computers. His back was to them and he didn't hear them come in.

"Hey Bradley," James said.

The man jumped and spun around. "Jesus, McManus," he muttered. "You scared the hell out of me."

James raised an eyebrow. "I stepped into the room and said hi."

Bradley was about Gabriella's height, with dark brown hair and sharp features. He narrowed his eyes and then looked at Gabriella. "Who's that?"

"New candidate for the open spot," James said. "This is my cousin, Gabriella."

"Your cousin? We're hiring cousins now?"

The implications were dripping from his voice and Gabriella tensed up, preparing for a confrontation. But James just looked at her and rolled his eyes.

"Nice to meet you," Gabriella said, deciding to just move forward.

She held out a hand, but Bradley was already turning back to the computer. "There's a situation at the reservoir," he said, clearly directing this at James. "I was going to go over this month's budget, but if you're with your...cousin, I'll take this one."

"Thanks, I appreciate that," James said. "You need any backup?"

"No, they're tapping us for early observations, nothing else. Plus it's probably bullshit. The Foundation knows it, but they have to check anyway."

"I'll keep my phone on. Call me if anything comes up."

Bradley nodded, still not facing them. Then he typed a couple more things, closed the browser window, and walked out of the room.

"Friend of yours?" Gabriella asked.

James shook his head. "He's good at his job, at least. And not always a total dick."

He led her over to the squashy blue couch. "Come on, sit down."

He sat on one end and picked up a coffee that was sitting on the side table. He took a sip and grimaced. "I forgot about it," he said, standing up. "Give me a sec, I just want to reheat this a little. You sure you don't want milk or anything?"

Maybe it was just nerves, but she felt like she'd look like a child changing her mind now. "No, I'm fine."

James walked back into the kitchen, leaving her alone in the living room. Gabriella looked around. She had to admit that up close, this room did look like some version of the central command center she'd been envisioning. The maps on the walls were marked up and there were notes on whiteboards referencing things she couldn't begin to comprehend. But the addition of the old fireplace and the knick-knacks on the shelves softened the room somewhat. She was even sure she recognized some things from Auntie Dana's house that James must have taken with him at some point.

"So," James said from beside her, causing her to jump and slosh her coffee. "I assume you have the general gist of what we do here, right?"

Gabriella nodded. "Yeah, standard paranormal stuff? Investigating, clearing, that kind of thing?"

"Yes, and no."

He sat down again and took a sip of his coffee. He winced. "Too hot now."

James set the coffee down on the table, using a coaster with a friendly-looking ghost drawn on it. "So yeah, we do those things.

Though we're generally the ones brought in to clean things up after the actual investigations have been done. So we're not going in to prove or disprove a haunting. That's been done by other people before we even get there. But we also do more in-depth stuff. More intense work."

"Like what?"

"Well, curses? Intelligent hauntings, not just echoes. Some more cryptozoological work-"

"Cryptozoological?" Gabriella repeated. "What, like Bigfoot?"

"That one was before my time," James said. "But yeah. Bigfoot. Things in the woods. Entities that can't be defined. Vampires."

Vampires. Crystals were one thing. Ghosts too. She'd grown up with that stuff and could handle it. But vampires? Gabriella set down her mug on the coffee table, shook her head, and stood up. "I've got shit to do," she said. "I don't know why you're fucking with me, but it's not cool."

CHAPTER 2

"No, wait!"

James reached up and grabbed Gabriella's arm. There was no trace of mischief on his face as she paused and turned back to look at him.

"Gabbie, I'm serious," he said. "Please sit down."

She sighed. "Why do you expect me to believe that?"

James shook his head, looking like the conversation had completely escaped him. "I mean, I'd hoped after everything at Gran's house..."

"Gran's house?" Gabriella repeated. "James, that was holy water and blessings, not vampires."

"We do those too," James said quickly. "There's actually a priest that works with us sometimes. Father McEnerney. You'll like him."

"What situation at Gran's could have possibly made you think I'd believe in vampires?"

James didn't answer right away. He frowned and furrowed his brow like he was thinking something through. Then he groaned and covered his eyes with his palm.

"Dammit, you would have been, like, seven. Of course you don't remember."

"Remember what?"

"Um, Uncle Tommy had that weekend camping trip out in Savoy? With his buddy and the bite marks?"

Gabriella stared at him blankly, but sat back down on the couch. "Um, no?"

James rubbed a hand over his eyes, shaking his head. "Shit, no wonder you think I'm messing with you. Your mom never told you?"

"No. Jesus, James, are you telling me there's a vampire out there that attacked Uncle Tommy?"

"It's not out there anymore. Uncle Tommy and Aunt Mary took care of that. But yeah, that's exactly what I'm saying. It got them at their campsite and bit his buddy. The guy lived, but he was never the same after."

Gabriella let out a long breath, then picked up her coffee and took a sip.

"That surprises me more than it should," she said finally.

"I thought they told the younger cousins about it," James said. "I was twenty at the time, but Aunt Mary wouldn't let me go with them. That's actually how I found out about the Foundation and North County Paranormal. Uncle Tommy's story had gotten back to them and they got in touch with him shortly after everything went down."

"And then you joined?"

"After college, yeah. The family knows about it but everyone's split between either treating it like any other job or pretending nothing ever happened. Uncle Pete still insists I'm working for a corporation in Boston."

"Yeah, I've heard him mention that," Gabriella said. "I thought it was a little weird."

"He's adamant I've been there for a decade now," James said with a shrug.

"Okay, so let's say I believe you," Gabriella said slowly.

She did, but she wanted to be sure she got all the details before agreeing to anything. Even with James. If they were talking about vampires, she needed all the information before filling out tax paperwork.

James perked up a little and looked at her. She looked into her mug of coffee, running a finger over the rim as she spoke. "So you fight vampires and cleanse houses. Got it. Is that what you're hiring me for? Or is there something more specific involved in this role?"

"That's the majority of it. Obviously everyone brings their own strengths to the role. But beyond Robin, who's our leader and Bradley, who oversees logistics, everyone is basically on equal footing. The primary focus is taking care of these things and keeping people safe."

"About that," Gabriella said. "How dangerous is this job?"

He grimaced. "It has its risks," he said. "I'll be fully upfront about that. We've had injuries, sometimes serious ones. You'll need to be in shape and there's a gym down in the basement that everyone has access to. But we've never lost anyone in this generation and we're very proud of that fact."

"Yeah, Mom's going to fucking kill you for hiring me."

James's face lit up. "So you're in?"

Gabriella nodded. "I need a job," she said. "And this sounds far better than anything else I might be able to get right now."

James grinned at her. "This is great!" he said. "It really is a great gig, I swear. And they will make sure you've got what you need to stay safe, don't worry."

"Who's they?"

"The Foundation. Little spooky, a lot mysterious, but they keep us funded. Everything we need in order to do the work is in this house. As you can see," he gestured toward the computer bank, "we've got tech, the gym downstairs, a full kitchen, first aid kits everywhere, and a few bedrooms. We tend to take multiple-day shifts, especially in the late fall and early winter. I'm not sure why that's our busy season, but there you go."

He finished his coffee and set the mug back down. Gabriella took a small sip of hers, trying to keep her excitement in check. This was starting to sound like a secret mission. In this high-tech headquarters disguised as a ranch home. Who wouldn't be excited?

"Do you have time this afternoon?" James asked. "I could give you the tour, introduce you to the rest of the crew. Whoever's around, that is."

"Sure!" Gabriella said. "I don't have anywhere to be."

"Great!"

He took their mugs into the kitchen and she followed, half expecting to see some high-tech hunting gear nestled among the coffee nook. But there was nothing out of the ordinary beyond one extraordinarily ugly fruit bowl and the rapidly browning bananas inside.

James followed her gaze. "Yeah, we've got a cleaning rota," he said. "Um, it's my turn."

He tossed the bananas in the trash, then swept a handful of crumbs off the breakfast bar and into the sink. "I'll do the rest later. Anyway, here's the kitchen."

A large fridge stood in the doorway and nearly every inch of counter space was filled with mugs and half filled grocery bags. Sunlight streamed in from between the sheer white curtains in the window over the sink, where a small vase of fake flowers sat.

"Depending who's on, we might do a family style dinner or it might be catch as catch can," James continued. "If you bring food, label it. Otherwise, everything in the fridge is up for grabs. They used to give us a food stipend, but cut that a little while back."

Gabriella nodded. Her usual routine of meal prep would probably keep working just fine.

"Alright, so down the hall here," James said, walking through the kitchen to the doorway and right down a short, dark hallway. "You've got the bedrooms and the bathroom. Bathroom's there. Again, it should be fully stocked. But if you're doing overnights, bring your toothbrush. We've had... issues with people forgetting whose toothbrush is whose and oh my God, I'm not dealing with that again."

The bathroom was an outdated cool green color all around. It was sparkling clean and there was an assortment of toiletries on the counter, including a bag with sample size makeup spilling out. The shower curtain was also green, but had the same friendly ghost as the coasters in the living room.

"Next, there's the three bedrooms. None are assigned, but Brad keeps a computer in that back room and everyone has their preferences. You don't have to work around those preferences, but if you want to actually get along with the people you'll be entrusting your life to, it can't hurt to be flexible."

"James, we're two of twenty-five cousins." Gabriella said. "I think we're both used to that."

"I'm just giving the tour."

He knocked on the closed door of the first bedroom. Nobody answered, so he opened it and stepped in.

Like the rest of the house, the bedroom was cramped. Two beds pressed against the pale gray wall with a single bedside table in between them. A large dresser took up part of the other wall, but that was the extent of the furnishings. The walls were nicely decorated and it gave off the vibe of a slightly more homey hotel room.

Beyond a beat up duffel bag on one bed, Gabriella didn't see any personal belongings. Right, she thought, it made sense that they'd treat this more like a dorm than anything.

James pointed at the duffel bag. "I'm on til Saturday, so that's my stuff."

"And you normally stay in here?"

"Yeah, unless anyone is dying for it." James said. "And we usually have a skeleton crew scheduled for overnights, so I'm usually alone or spending quality time with Bradley."

He started walking out the door and back toward the living room. Gabriella caught a glimpse of the bedroom across the hall as they passed. It looked exactly the same, just with light pink wallpaper instead.

"How many other people work here?" she asked.

James stopped for a second, counting. "Well, there's me. And Bradley, who you met. Robin is in and out. He's the captain of the team, so he also tends to liaison with the Foundation. And then there's Amelia, who let you in. And Madelyn. She got injured in the field last year, so she's just getting back to being on duty. And now you."

"Are there other groups too?"

"Yeah, the Foundation funds squads all over the state. Some places have bigger groups, but so far we've only needed the small group," James said. "It works out well. Everyone brings their own strengths to it. Oh, speaking of, let's head down to the gym."

Gabriella followed him downstairs to the basement. The stairs were plush blue carpet as they passed by the front door and came into a dark, narrow hallway. There were doors on both sides. One seemed to be silent behind it while behind the other, Gabriella could hear muffled pop-punk playing.

James pushed that door open and the music got louder as they stepped inside. Gym might have been a little generous, but it was still impressive enough by home standards. Two treadmills stood next to each other along one wall, underneath a line of small, propped-open windows. An exercise bike and a workout machine Gabriella didn't recognize lined the wall directly across from the door. A rack of free weights sat beside them, and the final wall was lined with mirrors.

"Everyone is expected to stay in shape," James said. "You don't need to be a marathon runner, but you do need to be able to get yourself out of a jam and help your teammates. I know you though, you'll be fine."

Gabriella nodded, stepping in to look at the equipment closer. They were the same things she would expect to see at her local gym. Where she could now cancel her membership.

"Oh, hey."

They both turned at the sound of a soft voice behind them. A woman was standing there, leaning against the rack of free weights. She was also maybe a few years older than Gabriella, twenty-four or twenty-five, with short, dark hair and dark eyes. A livid red scar ran over her right eye and Gabriella tried very hard not to show that she had noticed it.

"Hey, Madelyn," James said. "This is my cousin, Gabriella. She's joining the team."

"Nice to meet you," Madelyn said, holding out a hand.

Gabriella shook her hand and Madelyn smiled. "Welcome to the team," she said. "It's a great group."

"I'm excited to be here."

She was. Now that the shock of vampires had worn off somewhat, she was excited to learn more about what she'd be doing.

"What are you up to?" James asked Madelyn.

She nodded toward the treadmills. "I'm on for the weekend," she said. "So I wanted to get a couple miles in before anything pops up."

"Robin's not pushing you to run, is he?" James asked, his face suddenly concerned.

"No," Madelyn replied. "But I'm feeling pretty good today so I want to get some walking in at the very least."

"Good," James said. "Bradley went to check something at the reservoir. I'm going to check in with him in a minute."

"Are you overnight?" Madelyn asked.

"Yeah, just for tonight. So we'll be hanging out together tonight."

Madelyn laughed and started walking toward the treadmill. As she moved, Gabriella noticed a distinct limp and once again tried not to show she'd noticed it.

"We'll leave you to it," James said as Madelyn climbed onto the treadmill.

"Nice to meet you," Gabriella said.

"You too," Madelyn replied as they made their way out the door.

"She's a badass," James said a minute later as they walked back upstairs. "She got tossed off a roof last year and not only does she still come back, she hasn't even lost her enthusiasm for the work."

Gabriella felt her eyes widen. "A roof?" she asked, keeping her voice low. "What happened?"

"A case went wrong," James replied. "I can't go too far into detail right now, but we got bad information and she went in first. Thankfully, she lived."

They were quiet as they walked back up into the living room. The room was empty and James picked up their coffee cups and headed into the kitchen. "So what do you think?" he asked over his shoulder.

Gabriella smiled. "I think I'm ready to start whenever you'll have me."

CHAPTER 3

GABRIELLA WALKED UP THE walkway toward the front door of the North County Paranormal headquarters. She'd been up half the night last night, feeling like she had as a kid on Christmas Eve, jittery and excited and dreaming about what tomorrow would bring. While she had, like James said, grown up around the paranormal, she'd always been on the outskirts of anything Gran had done. Her mother protected her from getting involved in anything as a child, and then she'd gone away to college. This was her first time being right in the thick of it. So now she was practically running on that excitement as she arrived at her second day of work. That, plus the Redbull she was sipping as she made her way up from her car.

James had told her to come right in when she got here this morning. But as she climbed the steps, she still couldn't shake the feeling that she was walking uninvited into someone's house. The whiskey barrel full of flowers and the cheery welcome mat didn't make it anymore comfortable.

Gabriella stopped at the top of the stairs and hesitated. Should she just walk in? But what if James wasn't there and she walked in on a bunch of people she didn't know and who didn't know her? What if they kicked her out? She should just ring the doorbell.

But what if they thought she was too cautious for ringing the bell after joining the team? Or snotty, like she needed an engraved invitation in order to do her work. Maybe it was a test.

Oh God, it was definitely a test.

The door swung open, interrupting her internal agony. Bradley was standing there, an irritated look on his thin face. "Were you planning on coming in at any point?" he asked.

Before she could reply, he turned around and walked back into the house, leaving her standing on the porch with her face burning. Before the door could swing shut behind him, Gabriella hurried inside. She kicked off her shoes by the door and lined them up neatly beside the three other pairs currently sitting there.

She could hear two male voices coming from the living room right above her, but neither of them sounded like James. She walked up cautiously.

Bradley was now sitting on the couch, hunched over some papers on the coffee table. Another man with short, thin brown hair sat on the other couch with his back to her.

"I'm not saying it's not doable, boss," Bradley was saying. "I'm just saying it's extremely tricky."

The other man nodded, rubbing his fingers against his temples as Bradley pointed to something on the paper in front of him. "I can juggle it," Bradley continued. "Put off some of the tech repairs I've been planning and put that money toward paying that off. But then that puts us at risk of not having the tech when we need it. Or of it breaking down even more than it already is and costing more in the long run."

"Yes, Bradley, I'm aware of what happens when you don't fix your tech. I've been in charge for a while now."

The other man's voice was sharper than the sardonic tone Gabriella had quickly realized was Bradley's usual habit. She hung back at the top of the stairs, wondering if she should say something to let them know she was there.

Apparently unfazed, Bradley pulled the sheet back across the table and flipped it so that it was facing him. "Would they put us on a payment plan?"

"We're already on a payment plan," the other man said, pulling the sheet back in front of himself.

He scanned it for a few seconds while Bradley shifted on the couch and Gabriella continued to hang back awkwardly. "We need a bigger budget," Bradley said finally. "That's really all it comes down to."

"I've tried," the man, who must have been the Robin that James had mentioned, said. "The fighting it took just to get them to approve filling the empty position? Not a new position, mind you. The empty one that left us short staffed for over six months. That was like pulling teeth, and that was essential. The only reason they finally agreed to it was because it's in their own bylaws. They'll find ways to tell us that what we've got here isn't essential."

"Want me to talk to them?" Bradley asked.

"Absolutely not."

The words were out almost before Bradley was done speaking. Then the man turned in his seat and saw Gabriella. Now that she looked at him full-on, she could see that he was significantly older than everyone else she'd seen here, probably close to fifty years old. He had a thin, friendly face with a graying mustache and hazel eyes.

"Gabriella," he said, the word almost a question but not quite.

She nodded. Shit, she'd clearly been standing here too long. Now it was weird.

"Robin," the man said. "Hang on a sec, Bradley and I are just finishing up."

"Listen, I can make this work," Bradley said, the paper now in his hand. "It's going to be tight and we'll have to put off at least some of the repairs. But I can at least get this month's bill paid."

"Thank you," Robin said, standing up and picking up his coffee cup from the table. "I don't know, Bradley. Sometimes I wonder what it will take to get the Foundation to give us the resources we need. It's almost as though they've decided we're too good at this."

"I guess we should be fucking up more," Bradley said.

He stood up too, picking up his own empty cup. Then he walked out of the living room and into the kitchen, leaving Robin standing thoughtfully by the table. After a few seconds, Robin turned to face Gabriella, his worried expression melting into a broad smile.

"Gabriella, thank you so much for waiting," he said. "James told me you'd be by for your first day of training, but he had to run out on a quick errand with one of our other agents. So you'll be with me until he gets back. Nothing to worry about, nothing more terrifying than a large stack of paperwork."

He laughed, and Gabriella felt the knot in her stomach ease a little. "Take a seat," Robin said, gesturing toward the couch that Bradley had just vacated. "I'm just going to refresh this coffee, then I'll be back with the paperwork I'll need you to fill out. Would you like anything? Coffee? Water?"

"I'm all set," Gabriella said.

Robin nodded. "All right. I'll show you where everything is later, in case you change your mind."

He walked out, leaving her alone in the living room again. It was just like someone's grandparents' house. It could be her own grandparents' house, a cozy ranch house with a fireplace mantel stuffed full of family knick-knacks. The only thing missing was a grandfather clock chiming cheerfully in the corner. Even the calico cat snoozing on the windowsill was the same. If it weren't for the computers situated around the room, she could easily mix the two living rooms up.

She could hear voices coming from one of the bedrooms down the hall, but they were muffled, and neither sounded like James. Gabriella shifted a little. She worked here, she had to remind herself. She wasn't just a house guest overstaying her welcome. She actually worked for this organization now.

Gabriella glanced at the coffee table. Now that the papers from Bradley and Robin's meeting were gone, she could see a few textbooks scattered over its cluttered surface. *Introduction to Metaphysics* was facing her, its cover almost too faded to make out the graphics. The first aid guide beside it was much newer, as was the *Introduction to Calculus* book half hidden beneath a small notebook. Was she going to have to know calculus to do this job? Gabriella sincerely hoped not. She hadn't been awful at math in school, but it had been so long since she'd taken a math class that she wasn't sure she'd be able to keep up.

Bradley came around the corner again. Without saying a word to Gabriella, he walked up to the coffee table and picked up both the calculus book and the notebook. Then he nodded sharply at her and walked out of the room again. As he was going through the doorway, he passed by Robin, who walked in carrying a tray with a manila folder, two glasses of water, and a coffee.

"I know you said you didn't want anything, but I brought you a water," Robin said, handing her one of the glasses.

She could almost hear Bradley roll his eyes as he walked out of the room. Fine, whatever. She'd just have to avoid him as much as possible. It wasn't like she hadn't worked with assholes before.

"Thanks," she said to Robin, taking the water and taking a sip.

"So James tells me you two are cousins?" Robin asked as he sat down.

Gabriella nodded. "Yeah, I'm a lot younger than him, but our family is really tight. So I grew up with him there."

"That's wonderful," Robin said.

His voice seemed a little overenthusiastic, but maybe he was just trying too hard to connect with her. After all, James was supposed to be doing her orientation, right? Robin probably didn't spend much time making small talk with early twenty-somethings at this job.

"So you had a brief tour with him yesterday," Robin said. "Did he show you everything?"

"I think so?" Gabriella replied. "He showed me the kitchen and bedrooms and the gym downstairs."

"There's a little more to it than that, but no worries," Robin said. "I'll have him go more in-depth when he gets back. What else did you two discuss?"

"The basics, I guess," Gabriella said. "He said you're part of something called The Foundation? And it's not just ghosts, it's all different things."

"That about sums it up," Robin said with a laugh.

He took a sip of his coffee. "We're a branch of the Foundation for Paranormal Studies, the North Worcester county branch, to be precise. There are a number of branches around New England, all of which report back to the main Foundation in Boston. It's a good organization, respectable despite the focus on ghosts and goblins and things that go bump in the night."

He handed her the folder he'd brought in. "You'll find the handbook in there, as well as your employment paperwork," he said. "I think James told you that you'll get health benefits, effective immediately?"

"He did," Gabriella said, trying not to let the relief show in her voice.

"So if you can take a few moments to fill all this out, I'd appreciate it," Robin said. "And James should be back any time now. If he's not back by the time you finish the paperwork, you can start getting familiar with the handbook. We have a team meeting this afternoon, so we'll introduce you to the team then."

He stood up again and gestured toward a door she hadn't noticed before. It was just off of the attached dining room. "I have a bit of work to do in my office, but if you have any questions, just come knock."

"Thanks."

Robin smiled. "It's good to have you aboard, Gabriella. Gabby? Ella? Is there something else you prefer?"

"Gabriella is fine."

"Of course."

He walked away, opening the door and going inside. Gabriella caught a glimpse of a desk and an overstuffed bookshelf before he closed the door, leaving her alone in the living room.

If she'd been expecting anything exciting in the paperwork, she would have been disappointed. Despite the fact that she was signing on to fight vampires and shadow people, the paperwork wasn't really any different from the food service jobs she had worked during college. She breezed through it and was just putting her emergency contact information in one last time when the front door swung open and she heard voices on the landing.

"-swear it was rancid."

"It wasn't rancid, you just hit it in the wrong place and it exploded," a woman's voice was saying.

The smell made its way up the stairs before the newcomers did. Gabriella's eyes watered as she smelled decay and a sharp burning smell overtaking the smell of fresh air she'd been taking for granted seconds earlier.

"Hey, Gabriella," James called, and she realized the smell was coming from him. "Give me a few minutes to shower and I'll be out to get your orientation going."

Before she said anything, he darted down the hall and into the bathroom, the smell fading slightly as he left. The woman he'd walked in with was the same one who had let her in yesterday. She smiled at Gabriella. "Hey, Gabriella, right?" she said.

"Yeah."

"Welcome back."

Gabriella tried to hide the fact that she couldn't remember this woman's name, but apparently, it showed on her face. "Amelia," the woman said.

"Sorry," Gabriella said with a wince. "I'm trying to keep everyone's names in my head."

Amelia shrugged. "It's your first full day, give it time. No one's going to get mad. Not even Bradley."

Gabriella laughed, then immediately shot a look around the room to make sure he hadn't heard. Amelia noticed and smiled. "I have to go change," she said. "See you in a little while!"

She disappeared down the hallway, pulling her long brown hair out of its ponytail as she went. Something about Amelia put Gabriella at ease far more than Robin had. Not that Robin hadn't been friendly. In fact, he'd been a little too friendly. But Amelia's breezy kindness felt much more her speed. The other woman was probably twenty-five or so, somewhere between her and James's ages. Seeing that there was at least one other person under the age of thirty working here made her feel a little more confident.

She picked up the handbook and flipped through the first few pages. Again, it looked like any employee handbook she'd ever received. Come to work on time, fill out your time card, and don't wear open-toed shoes. If it wasn't for the heading *Required Cleansing Protocol: Physical and Spiritual* about six pages in, she wouldn't have seen anything she'd never seen at Domino's.

The cleansing protocols looked pretty simple. She'd have to find out where the emergency eyewash station was. And apparently, they were supposed to have a mobile medical kit in their vehicle. Gabriella imagined a sleek SUV filled with mysterious tech, though it'd need some kind of Red Sox bumper sticker so that it wouldn't stick out too much here in Leominster though.

"Sorry about that," James's voice interrupted her a few minutes later.

She jumped, nearly dropping the handbook. James was walking back into the room. His wet blond hair was dark against his head and he was back in jeans and a tee-shirt, thankfully no longer reeking of dead cryptid.

"It's no problem," Gabriella replied.

She flipped the handbook so the cover was facing him. "Just going over the handbook."

"Oh yeah, Bradley's masterpiece," James said, a trace of a smirk on his face. "Alright, speaking of, he's got an Orientation guide around here somewhere. It'll give us a checklist of things to go over."

He walked over to the computer bank and started shuffling through some piles of paper. "Where..."

"Filing cabinet A, bottom drawer."

Bradley had managed to come back into the room without either of them noticing. "And stop messing with my papers."

Gabriella thought James was going to say something, but he just rolled his eyes and went to the filing cabinet in question. "Thanks, Brad," he said.

Bradley narrowed his eyes, but didn't respond as he walked away.

CHAPTER 4

Two hours later, Gabriella's brain was so full of information that she worried it was leaking out her ears. They'd covered the computer system, safety protocols, exercise routine options, and the training modules she'd be required to complete. Even before she had opened module number one of one hundred, she was so overwhelmed that she was wondering if this was a mistake.

"Hey, are you alright?" James asked as she sat in front of the computer, willing herself to log into the program.

Gabriella nodded. "Yeah," she said. "Yeah, I'm fine."

James smiled gently and she was suddenly struck by the fact that he had their grandmother's smile. "Nah, you're completely overwhelmed," he said. "It's fine, it's your first day and I just threw a ton of information at you all at once."

"It's just a lot," she admitted. "Like, the fact that vampires exist is enough to swallow. But that there's a known nest of them in Westminster? It's a lot. And that computer system is so confusing and I don't think I'm in good enough shape to even start one of the easier routines."

She turned back to the computer and watched the little hourglass spin on the screen as the training program slowly loaded. It was fine. She just needed to take a breath and get started.

"Tell you what," James said, glancing at his watch. "It's almost one. How about we take a lunch break? These modules can wait until tomorrow, we still have more orienting to do. And don't worry, seriously. You're going to do fine, trust me. And I'll be here to help you."

Gabriella smiled, feeling a weight lift just a little. "Are you sure?"

"What, that I'll be here? Obviously."

"No, about stopping."

James laughed. "Oh my God, go take a break."

She stood up. "Thanks."

"Any time. Now go! Go get one of those Panera sandwiches or something."

She had to suppress a laugh as he waved her off, but also had to admit that sounded like a good plan.

"Alright, I'll be back in half an hour."

"An hour."

"Yes, Dad."

James laughed as she headed for the front door.

***

An hour later, Gabriella was walking back up the stairs and into the house. She felt better after a chicken sandwich and some time in the normalcy of Panera. Sitting in a booth among office workers and moms out with babies in their carriages, she could take a few minutes away from the ghosts and fears of her new job.

Not that she was a newcomer to the idea of ghosts. James had been right yesterday when he argued that growing up in Gran's house showed her the truth. Strange footsteps and whispering voices were just part of life, especially in the three years that Gabriella and her mother had spent living there with her. Gran had always had protections up all over the house, and every grandchild knew you didn't mess with them. And if Gran wanted to teach you about one, you shut up and you listened to her. Even though it had been five years since Gran's death, Gabriella knew her aunts kept all of Gran's charms exactly where she had left them.

But the fact that these things were no longer on the outskirts of her life was what made the whole thing so surreal. No, now all of those things were front and center. Mom was going to be so mad at her for inviting this shit in, as she was bound to say when she inevitably found out about Gabriella's new job.

Still sipping her mango green tea refill, Gabriella opened the door and kicked off her sneakers, leaving them beside a pair of worn boots. As she walked up the stairs, she could hear the sound of James laughing in the living room.

"The only thing that saved me is that the smell went away as soon as I got under the water," he was saying to Amelia, who was sitting on the couch near him. "I can't imagine what the guys would say if I went home still smelling like that tonight."

"You wouldn't be going home," Amelia replied. "They'd smell you coming up the street and lock you out immediately. You think Graham doesn't have everything set after last time?"

"Fair," James admitted. "But we got a new housemate and-oh, hey Gabs!"

"Hi," she said, coming into the room.

James and Amelia were both eating lunch. James had a turkey sub laid out on the coffee table while Amelia sat with some kind of grain bowl in her lap. She smiled at Gabriella. "How are you doing?" she asked.

"Good," Gabriella said. "Um, James has been going through the orientation book with me."

"Bradley's masterpiece," she said, taking a bite of tuna and lettuce.

James held up a finger, then swallowed the massive bite of turkey that was in his mouth. "Give me a couple minutes to finish up," he said. "Then we can get back to it."

"Don't hurry for me," Gabriella said. "I can, like..."

She faded off as she realized she had no clue what her alternative would be. Amelia moved over and beckoned her into the open space on the couch.

"Come sit down with us," she said. "We were just discussing the case this morning."

Gabriella sat down next to her. She knew she was sitting in a way that was awkwardly stiff, but she couldn't bring herself to the level of loose casualness that the other two had. Not yet. This was her first job that didn't involve a fryolator and she still wasn't sure the best way to act at it.

"What was the case?" she asked.

James and Amelia exchanged a look. "Well, it was originally a call about a shadow person over at a pizza place downtown," James said. "But when we got there, it wasn't a shadow person. Apparently, the guy that called the Foundation had been seeing the actual shadow of some other thing, I don't even fucking know what."

"So it was out snuffling at the dumpster out back in broad daylight," Amelia continued, digging through her bowl and stabbing a cucumber slice. "We go and check it out, but it's nowhere to be seen. And James lifts the lid to look inside."

"And Gabs, swear to God, I thought it was a giant squirrel or something," James said. "But it pops out and it startles me so bad that I drop the dumpster lid. It hits the thing on the top of the head. And it explodes."

"Like, when he says it explodes, it's like guts everywhere," Amelia continued, eating cheerfully despite the disgusting topic. "And I don't know if James has actually ever seen a squirrel before, because this thing was the size of a dog. But either way, it just kind of..."

She made a popping noise with her lips, then went back to eating her lunch. James laughed and shook his head. "So technically it's taken care of, I guess," he said. "So I can tell the Foundation that it's not part of their pattern."

"What pattern?" Gabriella asked, relaxing into the couch just a little.

"There's been a few houses we've investigated that have had some odd energy readings apparently," James said. "Nothing I've noticed in my own cleansings. But the Foundation has experts go over the data we send them. And between us and the crew over at Worcester Paranormal, they've seen some oddities. And they're trying to determine what might be causing them."

"So these haunted houses are uniquely haunted?" Gabriella asked.

James nodded. "Yeah, I guess that's one way to put it. But so far there's been two in Leominster over the past year and three in Worcester and the surrounding towns. It's weird because there's nothing we can do on our end except continue sending data. But it's not like they're giving us anything to go off of. I don't think they're extra dangerous, but a little more information would be useful in the field, you know?"

Amelia shrugged and huffed a laugh. "Typical," she said. "Are you surprised though?"

"Nope," James replied.

He ate the last bite of his sub, then crumpled up the wrapper and stood up. "Alright, I'm all set," he said. "Gabs, give me a second to wash my hands and we can get back to that orientation book."

He walked into the kitchen and a second later, she heard the sound of running water. Amelia picked up the lid to her bowl and clamped it tight. "I gotta go do some work," she said. "See you later."

Then she was out, leaving Gabriella alone in the living room for a second. The friendly ghost on the coaster in front of her smiled cheerfully at her as she picked the orientation guide back up and tried to find where they'd left off.

***

They held the meeting that afternoon in the living room. James and Gabriella had already been in there working through the orientation guide when Robin popped his head in and gave them a five-minute warning.

"This is just a housekeeping meeting," Robin said to Gabriella. "Sometimes we have to discuss upcoming cases, but other times we just have some updates from the Foundation. This is one of those meetings."

She nodded, feeling a little awkward. Robin smiled and disappeared back into his office while James set the orientation guide aside. "I guess we can be done with that," he said. "Read the rest of it later. But you've got the gist of what's going on in there?"

There were still about twenty pages left to go in the orientation guide. Gabriella was hoping James would go through them with her, but he seemed to be shifting his focus toward the meeting.

Amelia walked in a moment later and sat down on one of the couches. "Any idea what we're talking about?" she asked James.

He shrugged. "Nope, Robin said it's just some housekeeping."

Amelia nodded and settled back on the couch just as the other woman, Madelyn, walked into the room and sat down next to her. She looked at Gabriella and smiled. "Hi."

Madelyn's smile was small, but warm, and Gabriella smiled back. "Hi."

Madelyn and Amelia started talking quietly and Gabriella couldn't quite catch what they were talking about. She glanced over at James, who was watching their conversation with interest.

"No, no, no," he interrupted loudly. "Amelia's spreading shit again. It did not get in my mouth when it exploded, thank you very much. I managed to close it just in time."

The three of them started laughing and Gabriella smiled. The tightness of the group reminded her of her roommates in college. She hadn't been part of the group, but she'd always wanted to be part of that casual warmth they showed each other.

James winked at her and her heart swelled a little. "You remember Amelia, the filthy liar, and Madelyn, who instigates," he said, waving toward the women.

They both started protesting at once, but were interrupted by the other man, Bradley, walking into the room. He sat in a chair set a little ways back from the couches.

"And Bradley, of course," James said, moving his wave toward Bradley. "The life of the party."

Bradley was reading something on his phone. He didn't even bother looking up as he rolled his eyes. "I actually have work to do," he muttered.

"Team martyr," Amelia teased.

Whatever retort Bradley had in mind got cut off as Robin walked into the room. "Thank you for meeting quickly before the end of the day," he said as he pulled out a chair and sat down at the front of the room. "We have a couple of things to discuss, but first I want to welcome the newest member of our branch, Gabriella McManus."

Everyone turned to look at Gabriella and her face heated up as she awkwardly waved. James nudged her.

"Um, hi," she said.

"Gabriella's in training, so please help her out with anything she needs," Robin continued. "I'm not worried though, I think she's going to be great."

He gave her a warm smile and she smiled back, some of the awkward feeling melting away a little.

"Alright," Robin said, turning back to the rest of the group. "A couple updates. The Foundation asks that we submit all requisition forms together at the end of the month to save on postage. They've also asked us to remind staff that if you need to be reimbursed for payments made in the field, you need to send in your original receipt. It can't have any additional writing or markups on it. This includes blacking out other purchases from the same trip. Amelia, I know you were asking about that. Get a separate receipt or send the entire thing with a note saying what you need to have reimbursed."

Amelia and James exchanged a look, but neither said anything. Robin didn't seem to notice as he carried on.

"What else..." he murmured as he looked down at the paper in his hand. "There's a training coming up in August about advanced first aid for known cryptids. If you want to sign up, talk to me about it. It'll be held at Tully Lake."

This was how the rest of the meeting went. Robin provided updates that sounded alternatively mundane and extremely dangerous. The Foundation was reminding them to rotate supplies, but those supplies included deadly poisons. A team-building camp out was scheduled for this summer and there were only a few slots left if anyone wanted to sign up. And the apparently biannual reminder that teams are not to bring home any souvenirs from cases.

"Any questions?" Robin asked after wrapping up a brief statement from the Inner Cape Cod team on the start of vacation season and its impact on hauntings in the region.

Everyone shook their heads, so Robin motioned to Bradley, who was holding his own list. "Alright," Robin said. "I'll hand the floor over to Bradley then."

"Everyone clean up your own shit," Bradley said. "If I trip over one more pair of sneakers, I'm keeping them."

Amelia booed him and Madelyn scoffed silently. Bradley made a face, but kept going.

"Next," he said. "McManus."

Gabriella's head shot up. What did she do, she just started here?

Bradley apparently saw both her and James watching expectantly. "No, him," he said, gesturing toward James. "The one whose medical forms have needed to be updated for six months."

"I'll get them to you," James said.

"Hurry up," Bradley snapped.

He looked back down at his list. "McManus again."

They both looked at him. Bradley looked back up and groaned.

"Just use first names, Bradley," Robin said, an edge of impatience in his voice. "We'll be here all night."

Bradley sighed. "James," he snapped.

"Sir."

Bradley looked unamused. "I've been told to remind you that the Foundation does not reimburse mileage for private vehicles. So your request was denied."

"Of course it was," James muttered to Gabriella. "They sent me to a training in Maine while the rest of the team had a case. Guess how many official vehicles we have?"

He didn't seem to expect an answer as he turned back to Bradley, who was apparently done talking. Gabriella sat and listened as Robin wrapped up the meeting. This was all very dull and strict for an organization that fought monsters. But maybe that was what made them successful?

After the meeting ended, James turned to Gabriella as the others went their separate ways. "You can head out," he said. "Technically, your shift was over about an hour ago, so we'll make sure to mark your time card accurately so you get paid."

"Are you leaving too?" Gabriella asked.

"Nah, I'm doing a twenty-four-hour shift, so I'm sticking around. You'll get those soon enough, don't worry."

Gabriella wasn't sure if she found the idea scary or exciting. But she gave him a hug goodbye and headed out the door. The sun was setting and her entire body was exhausted. But even before she got to her car, she was excited to come back tomorrow.

CHAPTER 5

THE NEXT MORNING, GABRIELLA was feeling a little less over-whelmed as she sat down at the computer for her first training module. She'd brought her own coffee today, so she had a large iced coffee on one side of the keyboard and a notebook and pen ready on the other. After a solid night's sleep, this was feeling more like the first day of college than her entrance to a job that might potentially kill her.

James had told her to expect the modules to last an hour each. He'd also warned her not to try and rush through them. Despite the fact that there were a hundred of them, the orientation manual emphasized the fact that the information in these modules was critical to working for the Foundation. She'd have other reinforcements and practical training, but some of the information she'd learn here on the computer might mean the difference between life or death someday.

Today's schedule, as Robin had informed her, would be four modules in the morning. After that, Bradley would get her set up in the gym. While she wasn't exactly looking forward to four hours of classes, Gabriella dreaded that part just a little more. She hadn't seen Bradley since yesterday morning and she was sure he hadn't started feeling any friendlier toward her in that time.

But for now, it was nine o'clock in the morning and she was sitting at one of the computers in the living room area, waiting for it to boot up. The morning sun was coming in the bay windows and someone on the overnight shift last night had left one of the side windows open, letting in a cool breeze. According to her weather app, it was going to get hot today, but for now it was comfortable.

The fluffy calico cat she'd seen the other day came strolling into the room as the computer whirred and the screen remained black. As the cat sat down and peered at her, Gabriella leaned over and held out a hand. "Hi there."

The cat looked at her with big yellow-green eyes, then walked a few steps closer. Gabriella clicked her tongue, but the cat stayed where she was, clearly assessing the danger of her presence. Gabriella tried one last time, then turned back to the computer. The screen now showed a blue background and a message box.

ENTER PASSWORD

Crap, she didn't have one of those yet. Hopefully James or Robin would be in soon so that she could get one.

"Good morning!"

Amelia walked into the room and the cat went straight for her, rubbing herself on Amelia's legs. She reached down and scratched the cat behind the ears. "You met Fang?" she said.

"Kind of," Gabriella said. "She seems a little shy."

Amelia ran a hand down the Fang's back and the cat started purring. "She'll warm up to you, don't worry."

She walked over to the computer and looked at the screen. "Oh, did you get your password yet?" she asked.

Gabriella shook her head. "Hang on," Amelia said. "I'll go get Bradley."

Before Gabriella could tell her it was fine, she'd just wait, Amelia took off back toward the other end of the house, calling for Bradley. Turning back to the computer as though it might change its mind, she waited awkwardly in her chair for a moment as Fang looked at her.

A minute later, Amelia was back and she was being followed by Bradley, who was carrying a stack of notebooks. "They told you to do your training, but they didn't give you a password?" he asked, eyebrows raised.

Gabriella shook her head, feeling her face get hot again. This wasn't fair. She felt like she'd done something wrong and she hadn't even done anything at all yet.

Bradley motioned impatiently for her to move over. She slid aside in her chair and he stood by the computer, opening some kind of administrator program. The computer moved slowly, but a moment later he had the program open to a submission form.

"Choose a password," he said. "Make it hard enough that no one can guess it, but easy enough to remember. Don't forget it."

"What happens if I forget it?"

"It's gone forever."

"Bradley has to set up a new one and it takes thirty seconds," Amelia said, now holding a purring Fang in her arms.

"Bradley has better shit to do," Bradley muttered as he moved aside to let Gabriella enter her password.

She chose something quickly, watched it turn to asterisks on the form, then moved so he could come back. He typed in a few more things, then closed back out of the program.

"Try it now," he said.

They all waited for an uncomfortable minute while the spinning hourglass rolled on the screen. Just as Gabriella was ready to scream from the awkwardness, the message box popped back up. She typed in her password and a second later, a Welcome screen appeared.

"You're in," Bradley said.

"Thanks." Gabriella said.

He shrugged. "You should have had that yesterday."

He walked away, nodding to Fang as he went. Amelia rolled her eyes, then smiled at Gabriella. "I'm going downstairs to do my workout, but let me know if you need any help with anything."

"Thanks," Gabriella replied. "Um, I'll let you know."

Amelia dropped Fang, who took off past Robin's closed office door and toward the back of the house. Then she turned and walked downstairs. Once she'd left, Gabriella turned back to the program and clicked on Module One.

WELCOME TO THE FOUNDATION FOR PARANORMAL STUDIES. WE'RE GLAD YOU'RE HERE!

A clip art man shakily slid onto the screen, giving her a thumbs up. Then the monitor whirred for a second as he settled into place.

IN THIS FIRST MODULE, YOU WILL LEARN ABOUT THE MISSION OF THE FOUNDATION.

The screen blinked, and Gabriella felt a bolt of panic slide through her. Then it came back into focus.

YOUR LOCATION HAS BEEN PINPOINTED AS NEW BEDFORD. WELCOME TO SOUTH COAST PARANORMAL, A BRANCH OF THE FOUNDATION FOR PARANORMAL STUDIES.

Gabriella glanced outside. The same cheerful suburban neighborhood of Leominster she'd been in this morning seemed to smile back at her. No sign that she had been transported to the coast without realizing it. So apparently their GPS was about eighty miles off base.

The module continued much the same over the next hour. A PowerPoint presentation of the history of the Foundation, along with some fuzzy pictures, slowly chugged across her screen. Gabriella had a feeling that the problems were a combination of both the old computer and whatever out-of-date software they were running this module on.

The screen blinked out again as the focus shifted to the individual branches of the Foundation. But since the only line that made it on screen was, "New Bedford is historically a fishing port, meaning you'll likely deal with some cases on the water," she wasn't sure she was missing anything important.

The front door opened as she was logging back into her module in an attempt to finish it. Robin made his way up the stairs and headed toward her. "Good morning!" he said, his cheerful voice grating slightly on her frazzled nerves. "How's the first day of training going?"

"Not great," Gabriella admitted. "The computer keeps having problems, and it thinks I'm in New Bedford."

"We traded the South Coast branch for that computer," Robin said, setting down his briefcase on the coffee table. "Don't worry, we'll get you anything area-specific that you need to know later."

The computer made a grinding noise as the screen reappeared, then froze. "I have my laptop with me," Gabriella said. "Can I just do the modules on there?"

"Sorry," Robin said far too cheerfully. "Foundation policy is that you have to use their equipment. There's too much sensitive information to be opening on anything they aren't able to protect."

Gabriella was pretty certain that if anyone even thought about installing antivirus software on this computer, it would just melt. But she said nothing, and Robin clapped her on the shoulder. "Just try your best," he said. "Take your time."

With that he walked away toward his office, leaving Gabriella staring at a screen that was now blinking at her.

***

"So if there's anything more important than the training modules, it's your fitness routine."

Bradley and Gabriella were standing outside the gym, looking over a binder of exercise routines. The pages in the binder were old and contained graphics of buff men lifting weights and running in short shorts. After three hours of fighting with the training modules, Gabriella was dressed to exercise and ready to work out some of her anger on the treadmill. But apparently Bradley needed to give her a full orientation of the gym or something before she could do that. And based on the sour look on his face, this wasn't his idea.

"Nobody gives a shit what you look like, it's not about size," he continued. "But it is about how limber you are. How fast. You need to be able to get away from a dangerous situation. And you need to be able to get your teammates out of one too. Do you have any kind of workout routine going already?"

Gabriella nodded.

"Good," Bradley continued. "The Foundation requires us to follow these to an extent. But as long as you can do the things they need you to do, you don't need to actually follow them line for line every time. Got it?"

"Yeah."

He pushed open the door and they walked into the tiny gym. As they came in, Gabriella saw James was already in there, running on one of the treadmills. He was sweating through his tank top and had clearly been there a while. Even though he was wearing headphones, he looked up and gave them a wave.

Gabriella waved back. Bradley either didn't notice or ignored him. "Equipment is all here," he said. "You can do your workouts during work hours, but don't leave the property to go for a jog or something like that. We need everyone on call when they're on the clock."

Gabriella nodded. "And make sure you actually do the work," Bradley said. "There was a guy in the Foundation who died a few years ago on a case. He got caught under the corpse of a creature his team killed and wasn't strong enough to lift it off of himself. The thing's mate came by and tore him in half."

Gabriella felt the blood drain from her face. She was about to ask for more details, then immediately start bicep curls at thirty pound free weights. But then she heard James laughing from the treadmill.

"Are you really telling that bullshit story?" he asked, only slightly breathless as he slowed down and stopped running.

He got off the treadmill and came over to where they were standing. "Bradley's down here telling ghost stories," he said to Gabriella. "Just do your workouts, stay in shape. You'll be fine."

"You won't be saying it's bullshit when you get your head ripped off."

"You're the one telling the Foundation's oldest urban legend."

"Go wipe the treadmill down. It's got your sweat all over it."

James smirked, but he went over and pulled a paper towel off the rack and sprayed it with cleaner. He started wiping the treadmill he'd been using as Bradley walked over to the other one. Gabriella wanted to get started with her workout, but didn't want to be running side by side with Bradley, who was already speeding the treadmill up to a run. So instead, she walked over to the mat and began to warm up.

Maybe the story was bullshit, but it was certainly motivational bullshit.

CHAPTER 6

THE MUSIC WAS PLAYING loudly from Gabriella's laptop as she buttered her toast with one hand and took a sip of her coffee with the other. It was a chill indie mix she'd found online recently and had decided was now an essential part of her morning routine. The wellness and self-improvement site she'd been reading lately emphasized the importance of a relaxed, but steady morning routine. So now acoustic guitars and gravelly vocals filled the tiny studio apartment as she got ready for work.

She was about a week in now and was finally starting to feel like things were sliding into place. The modules were fine once she got over the frustration of the glitchy computer. It felt more like being back in school than anything. And she found that the workout routines Bradley had set her up with actually felt really good once she was doing them. The trick was apparently to get into work and just do them and get it over with, rather than try to motivate herself to go downstairs to the gym after a full day of training.

The toast now ready, she pulled over her kitchen stool and sat down to eat. She had about fifteen minutes until it was time to head over.

Then she'd work out for a little while, then sit down at the computer and try to bang out a few more of the learning modules before Robin came in with some new on-the-job training task for her.

She was in that in-between point, Gabriella realized. She was feeling like she was almost ready to be done with the modules, but not quite ready to go on a case with the team. But despite that hesitation, she could recognize the progress she'd already made in the past week.

The team seemed really good. Obviously, she and James had known each other her whole life, and she was quickly realizing that he had no work versus family life shields going on. He was exactly the same person at work that he was at family parties. She liked Robin too. He was a little dorky and maybe a bit of a hardass, but he was kind to her and seemed to really care about her progress. And Amelia and Madelyn seemed cool too, though she hadn't spent much time with them yet beyond saying hello. But Amelia was so friendly and she'd offered to tell Gabriella some stories she had from the Westminster vampire den at some point. And Madelyn was still pretty quiet. But there was something about her that drew Gabriella in, despite the fact that they hadn't really spoken more than a few words to each other.

And Bradley was just an asshole, apparently. But whatever, there was always going to be one, and she could just ignore him if she had to. And he was apparently an asshole to everybody, so it wasn't just her.

Her phone timer went off, signaling she had ten minutes to get out the door. Gabriella hopped up and walked over to the living room area of her apartment, leaving the coffee cup and plate on the counter. She'd get to them later. But now she needed to find her backpack and lunch and head off to work.

She opened the fridge and realized she'd forgotten to make her lunch last night. Oh well, she could just go to Panera again. She had a steady paycheck now, and it wasn't a major expense. So she could feel grateful for it today and be more careful tomorrow.

Gabriella found her jacket slung over the back of her desk chair and threw it on. A quick glance out the window showed her it was raining today, so she was going to need it. She slung it over her shoulders, grabbed her car keys out of the bowl on the desk, picked up her backpack, and headed out the door.

Her apartment was one of six units in a converted house right outside of downtown. It was a nice, quiet apartment building and she'd been living there for about six months now. She saw her neighbors enough to nod to them and say hello, but nobody was looking to be friends and that was exactly how she liked it right now. Sometimes she'd see the old man downstairs, but this morning, nobody was on the staircase heading outside or in the parking lot as she left. So she climbed into her dented Toyota, tossed her bag on the passenger seat, and turned the car on.

So this was what it was like to have a full-time job that was actually fulfilling, she thought as she pulled out of her parking space. While she wouldn't have said no to an extra hour of sleep, Gabriella was actually looking forward to being at work today. Everything she was learning was so interesting and this was a solid way in which she might actually be able to make a difference. Even if it was in a weird, paranormal kind of way. But someone needed to fight those vampires, right?

She pulled out of the small parking lot and started making her way down the quiet streets. It was raining and the patter of raindrops against the windshield blended with the morning news podcast she was listening to as she drove. It was nothing too eventful, but the mundanity of the moment felt like a nice break before she headed into the weirdness of the day.

***

Gabriella slipped into the headquarters, sliding the lock shut behind her. She couldn't see anyone upstairs, but she was pretty sure that James and Amelia had worked the overnight shift last night. "Good morning!" she called up.

Silence greeted her, so she just made her way downstairs instead.

She got to the bottom of the stairs and passed the silent closed door, which she'd just recently learned used to be a med bay. There was no medic on the team so the med bay hadn't actually been used in a while. They tended to just go to the emergency room or patch themselves up, depending on the severity of the situation. When Gabriella had asked James what had happened to the previous medic, he'd furrowed his brow and thought about it for a moment until he'd had to admit that he had no idea.

Rather than convert the room, the Foundation had left the med bay in place, abandoned except for the occasional trip to dig into the cabinets for gauze and rubbing alcohol. The door was always closed and Gabriella honestly found it a little creepy. So instead, she turned deliberately to the right and went into the gym.

She opened the gym door and was immediately greeted by the sound of loud pop punk. "Good morning!" she called over to Amelia and Madelyn, who were walking on the two treadmills.

"Morning!" Amelia called over.

Madelyn smiled and waved, then grimaced a little and slowed her pace. Gabriella went to set her bag down in the corner, then headed to the corner of the room and unrolled a yoga mat to begin stretching.

As she went through the somewhat mindless routine of warming up, she tried to mentally review what she'd learned in her modules yesterday. Everything she'd done had been focused on shadow people.

They looked like ghosts, but weren't. Frequently elicited feelings of fear and unrest in the people around them. Potentially drained energy or fed off of negative energy.

Or was that a different entity? Did shadow people feed off of fear or did they just create it? She'd have to review that quickly before the mini quiz at the end of the section. Either way, the rest of it she felt pretty secure with.

So today it was local geography and more incorporeal entities. And combinations of the two that would absolutely keep her from sleeping tonight. Since the system was still convinced she was doing her modules from New Bedford, James had had to improvise a more localized curriculum for her. This involved maps of the area, basic local history, and some illustrated guides to different monsters. All of which were drawn with large muscles and sharp teeth.

The music blared from a speaker set up by the weight racks, the power chords and nasally lyrics waking Gabriella up a little more as she finished stretching. She stood up, feeling a little looser, and headed for the exercise bike. Madelyn and Amelia were still on the treadmills as she made her way over.

"We're almost done," Amelia called over as Gabriella sat down on the bike and plugged in her program.

"Take your time," she said. "I'm doing a couple miles on this today, then weights. So I don't need the treadmill."

Madelyn flashed her a smile and started to say something. But whatever she was about to say was cut off as she cried out in pain. Gabriella watched in horror as Madelyn gasped and stumbled, nearly falling off the treadmill.

Amelia yanked the safety cord on Madelyn's machine, then her own, as she hopped off and caught Madelyn. "I got you," she said softly as she eased Madelyn off the treadmill and into a folding chair that was sitting nearby.

"Sorry," Madelyn muttered.

"Don't be sorry," Amelia said.

Gabriella was frozen on the bike, unsure what to do. They clearly didn't need her help and she didn't want to interfere, but she also didn't want to just ignore her new teammates.

"Do you need anything?" she asked finally, standing up.

Madelyn waved her off, panting slightly. "No, I'm good," she said between breaths. "Thanks though. James told you?"

Gabriella nodded. "Yeah," she said. "Some of it."

"I'm okay," Madelyn said. "Don't worry. And don't stop for me."

That seemed to be directed at both Gabriella and Amelia. Gabriella looked at Amelia, but Amelia was getting back on her treadmill. Madelyn noticed Gabriella's hesitation.

"It's fine, I swear," she said quietly. "I'm recovering, there's going to be setbacks."

Before Gabriella could say anything else, Madelyn eased herself carefully out of the chair and started walking slowly toward the exit, balancing herself against the wall as she went. The door closed behind her and Gabriella heard Amelia's treadmill starting up again.

"Don't worry," Amelia said. "For real, she's okay. Go finish your workout."

Gabriella turned back to the screen on the exercise bike and began to reset her workout, but the energy and enthusiasm she'd felt just a few minutes ago had dissipated somewhat. Instead, she now felt like an intruder on something well-established and personal. Trying to shove the feeling aside, she closed her eyes and threw herself into the workout.

Shadow people also showed up with hats on, she remembered as her blood started pumping. Usually fedoras.

***

"Hey."

Gabriella was coming back into the living room after her shower when Amelia stepped out of the kitchen. "Oh, hi," Gabriella said.

"Listen," Amelia started. "Madelyn's fine, so don't worry. What did James tell you about what happened?"

"Not much," Gabriella said. "It's not really my business, so I don't want to intrude."

"No, it's fine. Madelyn actually asked me to tell you. Last year we were on a case and there was this entity. We thought it was a shadow person, but it was material. And we chased it up to the roof. It threw Madelyn off and by some miracle she survived."

"Oh my god," Gabriella breathed.

"She's recovering and they've told her she'll basically always have some position in the Foundation, but it's a long road to recovery. So sometimes there'll be situations like today."

Gabriella wasn't quite sure how to respond, so she nodded. "Thanks for telling me," she said.

Amelia shrugged. "It was Madelyn's idea," she said. "Anyway, I'm making coffee and I know you're about to tackle some more of those modules. So what do you want in your coffee?"

CHAPTER 7

James had a wide smile on his face as Gabriella walked into the North County headquarters a few nights later. "You ready?" he asked her.

"Ready for what?"

"For your first field case?"

Gabriella stopped short next to the doorway, one shoe half off as she looked at him. "Seriously?"

James nodded, still grinning. "We've got something over on the Fitchburg line. Entities in an old house. The family got in touch with the Foundation and they want us over there. Should be a simple cleansing, maybe a little bit of shadow people action."

Had a gallon of adrenaline just dumped itself directly into her veins? Gabriella tried to pull her shoe back on, but her hands were shaking as she did so. "Um, yeah," she said, trying to slow her suddenly racing heart. "Yeah, great."

James clearly saw straight through her attempt at calm because he squeezed her shoulder as she stood back up. "It's going to be fine," he said. "You're going to be mostly observing tonight anyway. It'll be you, me, and Amelia in the field with Robin, Madelyn and Bradley supporting us from base. And seriously, it's like herbs and chanting. So don't be nervous, it's going to go great."

She nodded, unconvinced. But his easy smile made her feel better. That was the same face that had cheered her up after falling off the monkey bars as a kid or getting in a fight with her mom as a teenager. So if James said it would be fine, it was going to be fine.

A few minutes later, they were all sitting in the living room. Bradley had a presentation going on the computer monitor while the others sat on the couches like a strange Thanksgiving day football game scene.

"Alright, so the activity is primarily focused on the basement, but the owners report that there have been signs of it in the mudroom over here as well," Bradley said from behind the standing desk with his laptop on it.

He used the cursor to circle a section of the blueprint he was presenting. The basement was marked with several ghost emojis and as he clicked on the mudroom, another appeared there.

"I talked to Father McEnerney and he's on standby if we need him," Bradley continued, his voice all business despite the ghosts smiling on his screen. "But the Foundation says they think this is a pretty open and shut case. Their people went through and did all the energy readings and actual investigating. So we're just on cleanup duty. Any questions? No? Good."

Amelia had been starting to raise her hand, but she rolled her eyes and lowered it back down. Bradley ignored her. "Robin is apparently off tonight. He left the directions as well as the report from the Foundation."

"Robin's not here?" James asked.

Bradley gestured around the room with his eyebrows raised and James held up his hands in surrender. "Just asking, geez."

"He left me with all the prep work and apparently James is running the field team," Bradley said. "So let's just get this over with."

James stood up and went to the front of the room. "Thank you, Bradley, for that informative and charismatic presentation."

Gabriella shot a quick glance at Bradley, who was taking James's previous spot. He was very obviously ignoring James. Clearly not caring, James moved on.

"Okay," he said. "So two teams: field and support. Madelyn and Bradley are on home support tonight. Mads, how are you feeling?"

"Well enough to sit at a computer," Madelyn said, her voice surprisingly light.

"Don't push too hard," James said. "If you start feeling it's too much or you need to go lay down, tell Bradley. If and when that happens, Bradley's going to shut the fuck up and take over the task."

Bradley's eyes flashed, but James kept going. "Amelia and Gabriella are with me on the scene. Gab, you'll mostly be observing. Don't take notes, I know you're going to try. Just watch, jump in when you're comfortable doing so, and we can regroup at the end of the night."

Gabriella nodded, conscious of all the eyes on her. James nodded back. "A lot of it is going to be stuff the modules have covered, so keep an eye out and see what kinds of connections you can make to the training material," he continued. "Sounds hokey, but I swear it helps."

He turned toward the others. "Also," he said. "I want to take as many energy readings as possible while we're there. I don't know if this fits the Foundation's current pet project, but if there's some kind of strange energy crisis we need to be aware of later, I want the details as soon as possible."

"I'll be on visuals all night," Bradley said. "Send the energy readings straight to me and I can forward them off."

Amelia nodded. "Got it."

"Alright," James said. "Let's get packed up and head out."

He started walking toward the dining room-slash-prep station right off the living room and Gabriella got up to follow him. Several backpacks and piles of supplies were scattered over the long table in the center of the small room. On first glance, she could see several blades, a vial of holy water, and at least three pounds of salt in baggies.

Gabriella couldn't help but take a second to marvel at the fact that there was still a dining room table here at all. The kitchen she could understand, and even the living room furniture at least served a purpose. But keeping a dining room table in this room seemed like a commitment to the bit at this point. Why this strange blend of home furnishings and professional headquarters?

"What's up?"

James's voice broke her out of her thoughts. "Just looking at the table," Gabriella said with a small laugh. "I never expected a ghost hunting headquarters to look like Auntie Jen's house."

James laughed too. "Yeah, the Foundation bought the house at auction years ago with most of the furnishings still inside, and they just kind of stayed. I think like once a year we consider clearing it out, but Bradley just likes that taste of home a little too much."

"Or I know I'll be the only person actually doing any of the clearing out," Bradley snapped from behind them.

James smirked at Gabriella. "Anyway, let me help you get prepped," he said, ignoring Bradley. "Do you remember the module about house hauntings? What do you need to bring?"

Gabriella thought for a second, then picked up a vial of holy water and a pocket Bible. James nodded, then motioned for her to continue. She glanced at the table, then grabbed a small bag of salt.

"Good!" James said. "We'll get you a knife too."

Gabriella nodded as she put the supplies in a worn backpack. Then she zipped it shut and slung it over her shoulder. "Alright, I think I'm ready," she said.

***

After a few weeks on the job, Gabriella wasn't surprised when they got outside and climbed into an old black van instead of a sleek SUV. James slid into the driver's seat and Amelia silently offered Gabriella the shotgun seat. A fierce internal debate ensued in the next second as Gabriella tried to determine whether accepting or refusing would be the rude choice. Finally, Amelia decided for her by sliding the back door open and getting in.

"So this is our mobile headquarters," James said with a laugh as the van wheezed alive. "It gets us from point A to point B, but that's about it."

Gabriella glanced back into the middle and back rows of the van. Amelia sat in the middle with their backpacks beside her and the back seat had a few unidentifiable boxes stacked on it. But there didn't seem to be any kind of wild technology.

"It doesn't fly or anything," Amelia added. "In fact, it barely drives. But it's like the computers, we have to use Foundation property or we risk losing funding for it."

"Wait, they just won't pay?" Gabriella asked, turning forward in her seat.

James's smile was wry as he pulled onto the highway. "The Foundation cares about the work we do, but the main office cares almost even more about cutting costs."

"Which is ridiculous, they're loaded," Amelia added from the backseat. "They push this idea that they need to have money in the bank in case something big comes up. But, like..."

She gestured around them. "They literally give us exactly what they think we need and it doesn't get updated. So there's always too little money and noise about taking more away when we clearly don't need it."

"That's so weird," Gabriella said.

James shrugged. "That's them," he said. "Bradley does most of our admin work, including paying the bills. I don't know how he does it, but he manages."

Gabriella thought back to the conversation she'd accidentally witnessed between Bradley and Robin. How long could they last like that?

But that wasn't her problem to deal with right now. Here in this rattling van, she needed to prepare for her first professional house cleansing.

CHAPTER 8

Tiieir destination was an old Colonial-style house about fifteen minutes away from headquarters. The owners were gone when they arrived, so they stepped through the old screen door and into the mudroom, where they were greeted with stale stillness.

Had James said the family lived here? If it weren't for the hockey gear spread across the hallway and what looked like school books on the stairs, she might have thought it was empty. While there was plenty of stuff scattered around the house, the air just smelled and felt abandoned.

Gabriella glanced over at Amelia to see if she noticed anything odd about the air. Amelia was frowning, sniffing slightly. Then she turned to Gabriella and nodded in unspoken confirmation.

"Alright, so we're heading down to the cellar from here," James said. "And remember, we're not here looking for proof. That's already done, the Foundation's teams were in here twice and found all the evidence we saw back at the headquarters. So we're going to be going in here to cleanse it of what they found. So stay sharp and follow my lead."

Gabriella was slightly shaky with nerves and anticipation as she picked her way among the hockey gear. But James looked so calm and so in control that it helped to ground her. This was just another night at work for these guys. And eventually it would be the same way for her. So until then, she'd just have to fake it until she made it.

They made their way through the mudroom and James opened the front door. It led into a wide foyer that was littered with coats and shoes that had been tossed around, either by the owners or by the entity inside. Gabriella didn't like to think that something could be this aggressive, but she also couldn't see some parents picking up a kid's parka and tossing it on the staircase on their way out. Then she noticed that the air didn't smell quite so still in here.

"James," she whispered.

"What's up, Gabs?"

"This might sound kind of dramatic, but the mudroom. Did it smell-"

"Like a grave," James finished. "Yeah. Yeah, that's part of it."

"Wonderful."

Amelia huffed a laugh and James clapped her on the shoulder. "Don't worry," he said. "The report Robin left us said it's shadow people. Possibly some poltergeist activity. Shouldn't be anything more intense than that."

The foyer stretched forward into the kitchen. Again, the room was trashed. Something had tipped two garbage bins over and food scraps spilled over the linoleum. Gabriella pressed a hand to her nose. For such fresh-looking scraps, there was a really nasty odor in the room. The scent of rot made her eyes water, and underneath it, there was something else. Something that almost seemed malicious.

Amelia surveyed the kitchen with an even glance. "I'm going to assume that they didn't do this," she said, eyes on a stack of broken dishes still somehow evenly piled beside the sink.

As she spoke, a fragment of glass fell off the counter and shattered. "Nope," James said, shaking his head. "Nope, I'm inclined to agree with you on that. So much for it being contained to the mudroom and basement."

He turned to Gabriella, who was standing a couple feet back. "How are you doing?" he asked.

How was she doing? She was standing in a haunted house with her oldest cousin, about to go all Ghostbusters on the place. She was terrified, exhilarated, more excited than she'd been in years. And that didn't even begin to sum it all up.

"Fine," she said instead.

James gave her a long look and she smiled to convince him. "I mean it," she said. "I'm fine. I'm just going to hang back like you said to."

"Good."

He pulled out his phone, dialed a number, and waited with the phone held out in front of him. It rang for a second, then there was a click.

"How's it going?" Madelyn's voice said.

"Good," James said. "So far, at least. We're at the house and there are signs of activity all throughout the first floor as well."

"Yeah, the family said there were some in a later update that just arrived. I was about to call you," Madelyn said. "Hang on."

There was the sound of clicking and typing over James's speakerphone. "Dishes moving, weird smells. Sound familiar?" Madelyn asked.

"That's exactly what we're seeing here."

"I left a message with Robin to update him, but I haven't heard back yet," Madelyn said.

"It's his day off, don't worry about it," James said. "I've got it under control over here."

"Tell that to Bradley," Madelyn said. "I think he's called Robin three times in the past ten minutes."

"Am I on speaker?" James asked.

"Sure are."

"Bradley, give it a rest."

There was silence on the other end. Then Gabriella heard Bradley say something that was too far from the speaker to hear.

"Repeat that?" James asked.

"He says go do your job for once," Madelyn said.

"Roger that."

Amelia snickered, and Gabriella laughed a little too. "Alright, we're heading into the basement from here," James said. "Give me a minute to get my camera on."

He set down his backpack and unzipped it, rifling around inside for a second before pulling out a small camera on a strap. He untangled the strap, then took a second to get it connected to his chest.

"Alright, camera's on. Bradley, you got visual?"

There was a second of silence on the phone, then Bradley came back on. "What the hell happened to that trash?"

"It's just scraps," James started standing back up. "Our kitchen's been wor-oh."

The trash, which had been recognizable seconds before, was now covered in a layer of black flies. Gabriella's lunch started making its way back up her throat, but she swallowed it back down.

"That's disgusting," Amelia said. "Okay, that has to mean something else is in the house. I've seen plenty of poltergeists and that's not their M.O."

"Gabs," James said, his voice suddenly more serious. "Do you want to go wait out front? We might have to change the plan a little."

"No," she said quickly, despite her queasiness. "No, I should stay."

"Okay," James said. "But I need you to stay on guard. And if I tell you to get out, get out. We've done this before, there are rules in place for it. So we're not going into unknown territory. But we do need to be careful."

Gabriella tried to tamp down the spark of irritation at his words. She wasn't a kid, but he was right, she was still in training. So she just nodded. "Got it."

James smiled. "Good."

He picked his phone back up. "Alright, I'm going to stay on the line, but keep my phone on my belt. So if you need me, just talk to me."

"Got it," Madelyn said over the speaker.

James clipped his phone onto his belt, then turned to Amelia and Gabriella. "Alright, you ready to do this?" he asked.

Gabriella nodded. "Yeah."

Amelia grinned. "Let's do it."

James opened the basement door and Amelia saw the yawning darkness that swallowed the stairs just a few steps down. Were they going to go down in the dark? She knew that those ghost hunter shows always had them investigating in darkness, but maybe that was for added drama.

Then James flipped on the light, which should have made her feel relieved. But instead, she was just more queasy. A thick layer of spiderwebs coated the rough stone wall beside the stairs and the breeze coming from the dusty darkness below them felt heavy with something that she couldn't express, but knew she hated.

After a few seconds, James turned on his flashlight and shined it quickly over the space. It was a pretty ordinary-looking basement, aside from the heavy darkness that seemed to permeate it despite the sickly yellow light coming from the naked overhead bulb. A furnace in the corner, a hot water boiler beside it. A few boxes stacked up with Christmas lights spilling out. In the far corner, she could see what looked like it might have been a bar.

Had this basement been finished once? She couldn't even imagine it.

"Alright," James said, his voice a little lower now. "So this should be straightforward herbs, ritual chanting, and candles. Amelia, you've got the sage?"

She nodded. "Got the whole herb bundle right here."

"Excellent. You do your part. Gabriella, you take this."

He handed her a small bell. She took it in her hand, then looked at it for a moment without saying a word.

"I'm not messing with you," he said, as though he'd read her thoughts. "I know it looks weird, but bells are a potent magic when it comes to hauntings. Energy meets energy. So I want you to take this bell into the corners of the basement after Amelia goes through them with the herb bundle. And get the windows open as best you can so that whatever is in the house can get out. I think between those that and me saying the necessary prayers, we should be able to get the house back from whatever it claiming it. If that doesn't work, we'll call Father McEnerney in for a blessing."

"We're sure the Father isn't on his Vegas trip?" Amelia asked.

Gabriella heard Madelyn snort with laughter over James's phone. "Pretty sure that's next week," James said, a smile coming over his face. "Alright, come on. Bradley, you still got visuals?"

"Confirmed."

"Amelia, Gab, let's go."

Feeling ridiculous, Gabriella gripped her little bell and followed Amelia as she lit the sage bundle and headed for the nearest corner. She flicked on a flashlight, and Amelia gave her a grateful smile.

"You good?" Amelia asked as she reached up to pop open a small, dirty window.

Was her nervousness that obvious? "I'm good."

Amelia nodded and raised the sage, wafting the smoke into the dim corner of the basement. It smelled good, cleansing in a way that reminded Gabriella of the incense her grandmother always had burning in her home. As Amelia headed toward the next corner, smoke trailing behind her, Gabriella held up the little bell and began ringing it. The first peal was almost hesitant. James looked at her and before he could say a word, she swung it harder, letting out a much louder volley of chimes than she expected the tiny bell to be capable of.

James followed behind, chanting in Latin in a fluid, practiced tongue. Gabriella could pick out enough to tell that it was possibly a prayer. Not the Lord's prayer, but something similar enough.

Gabriella turned to face James and her heart dropped as she saw something moving in another corner of the basement. It looked human, but only just. It was shadowy and the limbs she could see were just a little too long as it slipped between the hot water heater and a shelf.

"J-James-" she started.

He didn't stop chanting, but she could see in his eyes that he knew exactly what she was talking about. He turned around as the figure appeared again, just for a second, then melted into the darkness.

"Keep going," Amelia said, her voice low under his loud stream of Latin. "I see it too, that's what we're here for. It'll leave as long as we stay calm and cast it out of the entire house."

Gabriella nodded, but couldn't help her gaze from darting around the basement, looking for any more signs of it. Even in the dim light, there were far too many shadows. But Amelia and James seemed to know what they were doing and she didn't want to get sent outside to wait. So she took a deep breath and rang the bell even harder.

Between the three of them, they brought this procession to each corner of the basement, gradually filling it with fragrant smoke that trailed out of the few open windows. The shadow figure didn't appear again, no matter how many times Gabriela accidentally looked into the darkness.

They stopped in the middle of the basement a little while later, and James paused his chanting. "Alright," he said. "Let's give that a little time. I've got a tincture to go on all the entrances, so give me a second to do that down here. Stay by the light."

He took a flashlight and disappeared into the far reach of the basement. Gabriella stayed silent and still as she and Amelia waited for him by the stairs. It smelled less like a grave down here than it had before, but she still didn't want to attract the attention of anything while James was finishing up. She could hear him moving around the corner, behind the furnace. Then, a moment later he came back out.

"Done," he said. "Let's head up and repeat the whole thing upstairs."

The kitchen still stunk like decay when they got up there and the scent was possibly a little stronger. Gabriella tried to ignore it. James looked confident, and she was just going to follow his lead. So a little while later, when they'd finally cleansed the last room in the house, she was relieved when he nodded, satisfied.

"I think it's good," he said. "I want to do a quick walk-through with an infrared camera to see if there're any signs of anything right now. And I've got some EVPs to check over when we get back. But other than that, I think we're good. Still open and shut despite the change in plans. Gab, want to come with me?"

Amelia was gathering things up to bring out to the car. Gabriella nodded. "Yeah," she said. "Yeah, I'll come too."

Her earlier fear had melted away when nothing bad had happened. So while she still felt a little nervous following James through the house, she no longer looked at every dark corner with apprehension.

Once James was done with his inspection, they walked outside and met with Amelia, who was standing on the porch, talking on the phone. "Just updated Bradley," she said. "He wants to meet with you to debrief, since Robin apparently never picked up his phone."

"Can't wait," James said. "Tell him I'm dropping you and Gab off at home first."

Gabriella started to protest, but he shook his head. "Don't worry, I've got the debrief. Nothing tops off a night of unholy spirits like a chat with Bradley. So go home and take a break, you earned it."

She knew there was no arguing with him, so rather than try, she got in the van and they pulled out of the driveway. The ride to her house was quick and peaceful, music playing over the radio as the three of them sat quietly.

A few minutes later, they pulled up in front of Gabriella's building. "See you tomorrow," James said as she opened the passenger door. "You did awesome tonight."

Gabriella smiled. "Thanks," she said. "I really liked it."

"Good, because you did great, and we're going to be doing a lot of them. Good night!"

She called goodnight to him and Amelia, then closed the door. He waited until she was walking in the front door, then she heard him pull away as the door swung shut.

Now that the adrenaline was fading away, Gabriella was exhausted. Shower first, then straight to bed. She had no idea what time it was, but it was dark outside, so that meant it was close enough to bedtime. The sun had gone down while they were at the house and she'd lost track of the time even before they'd gone down into the basement. The haunted basement where some kind of entity was lurking.

She ran back over the entire case as she scrubbed herself in the shower. It had been so simple. How could something so mysterious be handled by something so simple? She knew there had to be physics in there somewhere, some kind of order to the spirit world. But still, it was unreal to think that this was her new job.

The studio apartment was silent as she got out of the shower fifteen minutes later. Screw dinner, she'd just eat a big breakfast tomorrow. She was too tired to cook anything right now, and even her usual lazy dinner of Nutella from the jar sounded like too much work. Gabriella slid into bed, sighing with relief as she settled in beneath the sheets. She was exhausted, but satisfied. And excited for what tomorrow would bring.

With one last look around the room, she shut off the bedside lamp, plunging the apartment into a slightly pink-tinged darkness. She sighed again, then closed her eyes.

And that was when something reached up from under the bed and latched onto her arm.

CHAPTER 9

Gabriella knew she was dead the instant that icy hand clamped down on her arm. She had always thought in a situation like this, she'd scream and jerk away from whatever was holding her. Not that she'd spent a lot of time worrying about monsters under the bed since she was eight years old, but the possibility had always been there. And she'd always pictured herself breaking free and running away from the monster. But in the moment, all she could do was lie still and know with complete certainty that she was already dead.

Claws raked over her arm, and there was a flash of hot pain as her skin split. This was enough to break through the fatal fog she seemed to be in. Her mind suddenly cleared, Gabriella ripped her arm away. She swallowed a scream at the feeling of the skin ripping further as she wrenched it away from the claws, then rolled over to see what had her. In the pink glow of the room, she saw an arm slide back under the bed and out of sight.

It was too fast, too fluid to be anything natural.

Tears streaming down her face from both pain and fear, Gabriella reached for her phone. Normally she fell asleep listening to music, so it was always sitting right beside her pillow. But as her hand grasped empty air, she realized with sinking horror that her phone was on its charger across the room.

Damn that productivity and wellness website. This had been a terrible week to start that new bedtime routine.

Gabriella took a deep breath and tried to stay calm. She needed to get to her phone. Once she got to her phone, she could call James and he'd come help her. It was just another case. She happened to be a rookie with no supplies on her. Which made this case even more difficult. But just a case. She'd done fine tonight, she just needed to do fine for a little while longer.

What would James tell her to do right now? Or Robin? She took another breath, trying not to move the bed too much as she attempted to stop trembling. They'd say to stay calm. It was just like tonight at the house. The plan changed, but there was still a plan in place. She just needed to stay calm and follow it.

She shifted as silently as possible on the bed and heard something echo that movement underneath her. Okay, first she needed to reach the lamp on her bedside table. The light probably wouldn't get rid of the monster, but it would at least give her the ability to see what was happening and maybe scare it a little. The pink glow in her apartment was usually comforting and cozy at night, but right now it was just dangerous.

Holding her breath and not moving any other muscles in her body, Gabriella reached out toward the lamp. She was flat on her back, arm dripping hot blood onto the pillow as she moved it. The searing pain was almost too much for her to handle, but the alternative was rolling over to use the other hand and alerting the monster. Then it would know exactly what she was doing and strike again.

Her trembling hand finally brushed the cool base of the lamp. Encouraged, Gabriella ran her palm up the body of the lamp toward the switch, listening desperately for any sound around her. A low, guttural growl, something she felt more than heard, vibrated up through the bed and she swallowed a sob.

She couldn't have brought at least the salt in with her? Gabriella had left the bag of supplies in the car with James and thought nothing of it. Nope, never again. If she survived this, she was going to keep her own bag at home at all times.

James. She needed to reach James. He'd be able to fix this.

But first, the light.

With a barely whispered prayer to nobody in particular, Gabriella flipped the switch under her thumb. There was a click, and a beat where she held her breath. Then the room filled with a golden light just as a window shattered on the other side of her.

Not bothering to suppress this scream, Gabriella jumped and whirled around in time to see a shadowy figure slide back underneath the other side of the bed.

Her phone was charging on the table next to the breakfast dishes she'd left there before work. It was maybe six steps away from the bed, which was fine. She could make it six steps right? And it wasn't like the thing didn't know she was up here. There was no element of surprise to be had here for either of them.

Gabriella took a breath, then let it out slowly.

One.

Two...

Before she mentally got to three, she darted off the bed and over to the phone. Barely stopping to pull it off the charger, she grabbed it and flew out the front door of her apartment, slamming it shut behind her.

Breathing shakily and not even trying to keep in her sobs anymore, Gabriella held the knob in place with her good hand. There was no movement behind the door yet, but the cheap doors in this building wouldn't be enough to keep anything in for long if it really wanted to get out.

When a few seconds had passed without any kind of fight, Gabriella let go of the door, looking for something, anything, to block it. There was nothing in this dim, dusty hallway that would offer even the illusion of protection. Now crying in fear and frustration, she pulled out her phone, monitoring the door for the creature. After a few false starts, she finally got James's number and heard it begin to ring on the other end.

"Hey, Gabs, what's up?" James asked easily as he picked up her call. "Just wrapped up with Brad and-"

"James," she choked out. "James, oh God, it's in my apartment."

She heard the sound of him standing up. "What's in your apartment?" he asked, voice now deadly serious. "And are you okay?"

"The thing from tonight, I think it followed me home," Gabriella said, the words coming out in a rush as she watched the front door for any signs of life.

"Are you okay?" he asked again.

Her arm was throbbing, and the blood was soaking through her t-shirt as she clutched it tightly to her chest. "It got me in the arm but I'm not too bad," she said, trying to keep her voice steady.

"And where are you now?"

As James spoke, she heard a door opening on his end, then footsteps on pavement. He must have still been at the headquarters when she called.

"I'm outside my apartment in the hallway."

"Do you have any salt?"

"No."

She felt foolish and under prepared, but James just kept talking. "Okay," he said. "Here's what you do. I'll be there in ten minutes. You wait there. I'm sorry to put this on you, but you need to make sure it doesn't leave the apartment. This thing is the Foundation's responsibility and we're on our way to help you with it."

"How do I keep it in the apartment?"

James didn't answer, and she heard the sound of his car starting up. "James," she repeated, unable to keep the edge of panic out of her voice. "How do I keep it in the apartment?"

James was quiet for a second, then he sighed. "Just watch for it," he said. "And tell us if it leaves. I guess there's really nothing else you can do right now."

She knew he didn't mean to make her feel small when he said it, but even despite her fear and pain, she felt that shame sparking low in her stomach. She really was helpless right now, wasn't she? She'd been doing this for over a week now. Yeah, it wasn't that long, but she should have been able to do something. What if there was something in her training that she just wasn't thinking of right now?

And who didn't have salt in their apartment? Did she have a shaker sitting in the cabinet? Would it have made any difference?

The ten minutes seemed to stretch into hours as she stared at the silent door, silently yelling at herself and watching for any signs of movement behind it. James stayed on the line with her as he drove, so she could hear him and whoever else was with him getting closer.

She was in her shorts and a crappy college t-shirt right now. They were all going to see her terrible sleepwear. But small favors, at least she hadn't decided to sleep naked tonight.

There was a monster in her apartment. Was that really what she should be concerned with right now? There were five other units in this building, what if it tried to go after her neighbors too? Could she do anything about it? Probably not.

The door didn't move the entire excruciating time she waited for the others to get there. Finally, she heard the building's front door open and a rush of footsteps hurrying up the stairs.

"Gabbie!"

James grabbed her and gripped her in a tight hug. Her injured arm scraped against his jacket and she hissed in pain, but still huddled up to him, trying not to shake too hard. Then James stepped back and looked at her. "Shit, Gab, that's a lot of blood."

Gabriella looked at her arm, which was still tightly pressed against her chest. "It grabbed me," she said.

As she said the words, the reality of the situation seemed to slide back over her. There was a monster in her apartment. It got there without her knowledge and it tried to kill her. This was a real thing that had just happened to her.

How had it even gotten there? Did it attach itself to her somehow on the way home? She hadn't seen much of it, but it had looked like the same thing they had gotten in the house, a shadowy, malevolent presence. It had to be the same one. But what mistake had she made that resulted in it following her home?

James gently took her injured arm and looked at it in the dim light. "Shit," he said again. "This looks like it's going to need stitches. Bradley, can you bring her to the emergency room? Me, Madelyn, and Amelia will take this."

The whole team was there, apparently. Except Robin, who was still on his day off. Madelyn was leaning on a cane a little further down the stairs, but Bradley and Amelia had just run up right behind James.

Bradley stepped forward and took her arm brusquely. She flinched, then relaxed slightly as he more gently examined the cuts. "Yeah," he agreed. "Come on, Gabriella."

"We'll take care of this," James said. "Don't worry, Gabs. It'll be fine."

She nodded shakily and started to follow Bradley down the stairs. As she passed Madelyn, the other woman put a comforting hand on her good shoulder.

"It's okay," she said softly. "We'll take care of it."

Gabriella nodded, feeling tears burning her eyes again. Bradley said nothing, just continued to lead the way outside.

CHAPTER 10

GABRIELLA FOLLOWED BRADLEY OUT into the cool night air and over to the van, which was parked haphazardly on the sidewalk outside of her building. Bradley hopped into the driver's seat and started the car as Gabriella fumbled with the passenger door for a moment. Even her good hand was shaking so much that it took a couple tries to pull it open. But finally, she managed it, then slid into the seat.

"I'll have to drop you off," Bradley said as he backed out of the parking space and headed for the road. "And you'll need to give me your key so we can lock up afterward. You're going to spend the night at headquarters after this, at least for tonight. We need to do a thorough investigation of your apartment. Maybe the whole building."

His cool professionalism was obnoxious on one level and comforting on another. "It was the thing from tonight," she whispered.

"No, it wasn't."

He didn't even look away from the road or change his stance at all. "Are you sure?" she asked. "You didn't see it."

"No, but it's not the same thing. The entity you investigated tonight is gone."

She was too tired to argue, so instead, she just nodded and sat back in her seat, watching the traffic passing by them. It seemed so late, but apparently the rest of the world was just going about their lives like a shadow creature hadn't just tried to kill her in her own bed.

As they drove silently down a long, tree-lined street, she wished that James had been the one to drive her to the hospital instead of Bradley. The other man wasn't being aggressive or dickish this time, but she could use some affection instead of cool detachment. And she'd only known him for a couple weeks, but she wasn't about to ask Bradley for any of that.

So instead she waited quietly as he finally pulled into the hospital parking lot and turned off the van. "I'll walk you in," he said.

"That's not-"

"No, I need to talk to the registration desk."

Bradley reached over, and for a wild moment, she thought he was about to hug her. Then reached behind her seat and pulled out a small bath towel.

"For the waiting room," he said, handing it to her.

"Right," she said. "Um, thanks."

He got out of the car, then came over and opened her door before turning and walking toward the emergency room entrance. Gabriella scrambled out of the passenger seat, her arm throbbing as fresh blood soaked into the towel he'd given her. By the time she was out and moving, he was halfway to the entrance, so she hurried to catch up.

The emergency room waiting room wasn't packed, but it was busy for so late at night on a weekday. Gabriella and Bradley got in line behind an elderly woman who was leaning on a young man's shoulder for support. As the pair ahead of them were walking up to the next available receptionist, an older woman poked her head out from behind the desk. "Bradley," she called, gesturing them over.

Gabriella looked up at Bradley, but he didn't seem surprised. Instead, he led her over to the woman's station. "Did it occur on the job?" the woman asked.

"Yeah."

"Anything I should know?"

"I'm not a hundred percent sure on the entity," Bradley said. "The injury came from claws, right?"

The question was directed at Gabriella. She jerked out of her daze. "Wha-um, yeah. Yeah, it clawed me."

The woman nodded, typing something into her computer. "And insurance information?"

"I haven't gotten my card yet," Gabriella said.

"No problem, hon," the woman said with a warm smile. "I'll talk to the Foundation's insurance department."

Gabriella shouldn't have been surprised that the Foundation had something as mundane as an insurance department. Who else would handle insurance claims? Santa Claus?

The woman took her information, got her a plastic wristband, and sent her to sit down and wait. As they walked away from the registration desk, Bradley fished out the van keys. "One of us will come pick you up when you're done," he said. "Sorry to leave, but I have to go and rejoin the others."

Wow, an apology. Maybe this was his version of comfort.

"It's fine."

Her voice sounded small and scared and she hated herself for it for a second.

"I don't have my key," she murmured, as she shakily sat down in the nearest plastic chair.

"Do you know where it is?" Bradley asked.

"Backpack by my bed."

He nodded. "I'll get it from there," he said. "What's going to happen from here is that we'll start a cleansing tonight if they haven't already. Then the Foundation will decide what has to happen next. You'll stay at headquarters tonight while they take care of it. Do you need anything from the apartment?"

She shook her head. "I've got spare clothes at Headquarters."

There were plenty of things she could use from her apartment, like a toothbrush or a phone charger. But she couldn't get her thoughts together enough to make a list. And if there was still a monster in her apartment, she didn't need the rest of the team taking the time to go through her stuff for her and risk getting hurt.

"Good," Bradley said. "Good luck. Call us when you're done."

With that, he headed for the door. Gabriella watched as he walked past the window and disappeared into the dark parking lot. Then she turned and made her way to the nearest seat for what she knew was going to be a long wait.

***

Five hours later, Gabriella was leaving the emergency room with her arm freshly bandaged. It had thankfully been a clean cut. She'd needed a few stitches, but not the amount she'd been dreading. The doctor let her go with a prescription for antibiotics and instructions to take it easy for a few days. So now here she was, drained on painkillers and lack of sleep, waiting for someone to pick her up and bring her to the headquarters for the night.

James had answered the phone immediately when she called him. He said that it seemed to have worked, whatever they did in the apartment to get rid of the entity. But in the morning he wanted to get Father McEnerney in there to give the place a blessing before Gabriella went back inside. She'd had a wild image of a withered, white-haired priest chanting in Latin over her Lululemon yoga pants and had needed to force the hysterical laughter back down before it escaped.

It was three in the morning, and the parking lot was quiet as she sat on a bench outside and waited. It wasn't completely silent, thankfully. There were a few cars pulling softly through the floodlights, their lights cutting through the darkness as they rounded the corner and left the parking lot. Meanwhile, two other patients had walked out of the emergency room in the time she'd been here waiting. The signs of life were comforting as she waited with a water bottle in hand.

She sipped from the water bottle, then took a deep breath of night air and sighed. Maybe it was the drugs or the exhaustion, but there was a dreamy edge to the world right now. Had she really just spent the evening in the hospital because there was a monster in her house? How had her life reached this point? Two years ago she'd been studying communications in college, thinking vaguely of working in public relations someday. And now she was fighting monsters? What the hell?

Finally, the Foundation van pulled up to the curb in front of her. The front passenger window was open and she could see James was alone in the car. He leaned over and opened the door for her. "Hey, Gabs," he said, eyes tired.

"Hi."

She climbed carefully into the passenger seat, noting that the bloodstains from earlier appeared to be gone. Had someone seriously scrubbed the car already? And after everything that had happened tonight?

"Are you okay?" James asked.

She nodded and saw his eyes flicker over the tightly wrapped gauze on her arm as she buckled her seatbelt. "I'm sorry," he said.

She shrugged, then winced. "Not your fault."

He didn't say anything to that, but she was too tired to think too much about it. So she leaned back in the seat, closed her eyes, and dozed as he pulled out and began driving again.

"Me and Madelyn are on the overnight shift," James said after a few minutes of silence. "She's been trying to get in touch with Robin, but so far we haven't been able to reach him. So hopefully he'll be back tomorrow and we can talk to him about extra protection for your apartment. I don't imagine you'll want to stay at the Headquarters permanently."

As much as the idea of going home terrified Gabriella, the idea of living at work was almost equally unappealing. Tonight she was grateful for the extra protection and the space from her apartment. But she lived alone for a reason. She wanted to have her own space and her privacy.

"Would you maybe want to go stay with your mom?" James asked.

"She's moving," Gabriella said, eyes still closed.

"Oh, I didn't know that."

"Yeah."

"Where to?"

"New Hampshire."

"Oh, nice."

They lapsed into silence as James pulled onto a main road and began to speed up the van. Gabriella opened her eyes and gazed out the window at the dark businesses passing by. What else was hiding in them? If her little studio apartment could contain a murderous shadow entity, so could that hardware store. Or that Mexican restaurant. Or that house where three college-age boys were drinking on the porch. What if those boys went inside tonight and were torn to shreds by a demon?

This really was an endless job, wasn't it? All they could do was try to keep everything under control and hope that things worked out. As she dozed off to the sound of the car's creaking motor, Gabriella wondered briefly how Robin hadn't gone insane yet trying to contain all of these problems.

CHAPTER 11

When Gabriella climbed into bed in the pink bedroom at Headquarters, lights on and the door wide open to the hallway, she didn't think there was any way she would sleep that night. But before she knew it, the sun was streaming in an unfamiliar window and she was staring up at the ceiling, trying to shake off vaguely remembered nightmares.

Right, the monster under her bed. That part had been real, she thought as the pain radiating through her arm caught her attention. The doctors had given her cream and medicine for it, but right now it was searing hot against the bandages.

The thing had been in her house. Her. House. She should have protected herself better, should have been able to avoid it altogether. How had she been here a week already and not realized she needed to protect herself at home too?

She glanced over at her phone on the bedside table and saw that it was seven in the morning. So she'd gotten a few hours of sleep, but it still felt like maybe she should try to sleep a little more. The room was peaceful and comfortable, which took away some of the weirdness of the fact that she was technically at work right now.

Like the rest of the house, this bedroom still held a lot of the signs that it was previously part of someone's family home at one point. There were paintings on the pale pink walls and ivy borders around the tops of the walls. She was in one of the two twin beds while the other was neatly made beside her. The decorations and bedding were charmingly mismatched, and she wondered vaguely if that had been intentional or if they'd just ended up this way.

Gabriella could hear someone moving around down the hall. James had told her that he and Madelyn were on the overnight shift, so it was probably one of them. James had offered to stay in the room with her, but she told him she was alright. This place had more security - paranormal and otherwise - than she'd ever seen in her life. So while she was still nervous, she didn't want him to feel like he had to babysit her.

After tossing and turning for a little longer, Gabriella surrendered and sat up. She wasn't getting back to sleep, no matter how tired she was. So she stood up and walked over to one of the small dressers, where the change of clothes James had suggested she leave here were neatly folded. She wished for a toothbrush and something a little more comfortable than jeans, but at least she wasn't putting back on the dirty, bloody clothes she'd arrived in.

She decided to shower before doing anything, since no one except James and maybe Madelyn seemed to be there. Gathering up her clothes and a towel, she opened the bedroom door and walked out.

Robin was walking down the hall as soon as she stepped out. His thin face winced in sympathy as he took in her injury.

"Gabriella, I am so sorry."

He looked genuinely upset as he looked first at the injury, then into her eyes. "This should never have happened, especially right after your first case."

"I'm alright," she said, shifting a little on her feet.

She was in borrowed pajamas in front of her boss. No matter how kind he was being right now, she really just wanted to get in the shower and try to wash away the grime and the pounding headache that was forming behind her forehead.

"I mean it," he continued, voice still warm and sad. "This should not have happened. James should have been more prepared and paid better attention to what was going on."

Gabriella frowned, her whole body suddenly cold. "What do you mean?"

"That creature was able to latch on to you and come home to your apartment without anyone knowing," Robin explained, his voice soft. "If James had done the recitations properly and actually followed procedure, you wouldn't have been hurt."

"What? No, James-"

"It was the same creature, Gabriella," he said, barreling over her protests. "It got out because James cut corners. I know he didn't mean to hurt you, but he did. And that is inexcusable."

Could Robin be serious right now? He didn't have any reason to lie to her about this, so why would he? She trusted James, but sometimes he didn't think things through, right? Hadn't Gran said that?

And Robin hadn't given her any reason not to trust him. He was the team leader. His whole job was to keep them safe. It wasn't like he was out to get James or anything like that.

"He didn't mean to hurt you," Robin continued as Gabriella's stomach sank. "Obviously, we all know how much he loves you. But if he hadn't gotten lazy with the ritual, none of this would have happened."

She felt tears pricking her eyes and she tried to blink them away. Even after a few hours of sleep, Gabriella still felt off-kilter as she looked at Robin and that headache was just growing. "I'll be talking to him today," Robin said. "It's inexcusable that you got hurt."

"Thanks," she breathed.

She didn't know the ritual James had done. All she knew was that she'd left that house and gone home to a monster under her bed. So for all she knew, Robin was right. And like he said, James would never intentionally hurt her. She knew that. But she was so sore and so rattled by everything that had happened, and there was no other reasonable explanation for how the entity had made its way from the case to her apartment.

"Alright, go take a shower and get some breakfast," Robin said, voice still warm. "The rest of the team is coming in for a meeting at eight."

He clapped her on her good shoulder, then walked past her and back out toward the living room.

In a daze, Gabriella walked into the bathroom and turned on the shower. Once the water was set as hot as it would go, she gave it a moment to warm up as she gingerly got undressed. As she climbed in, she realized there was no comfortable way to wash her hair without getting her bandages wet. So she awkwardly scrubbed it with one hand as she let the other bandaged arm dangle out from behind the shower curtain.

She tilted her head back into the stream and thought back to last night as the shampoo ran down her long hair. They'd gone in and done the incense, bells, and prayer. Was there something else that they were supposed to do? Some kind of protection that they'd missed? No one on the team had mentioned anything, but there had been a point when James went off by himself. Maybe something had happened then? Or maybe he'd just forgotten something. When they were at the house, Bradley had told him to do his job for once. Was there something more to that than Bradley just being a prick?

It took about twenty minutes under the hot spray until she felt a little more human and finally clean. By the time she got out, her head felt a little clearer than it had since last night. She slowly got dressed and realized she was dreading this team meeting.

How could James have been so careless? Obviously, he didn't mean to get her hurt, but that was what had happened. What other explanation was there? That they'd taken care of the monster and then an identical one coincidentally ended up in her apartment immediately after? The most obvious solution was the simplest one. And the most obvious solution here was that James had messed up on the case. And whether he'd done it deliberately or whether he'd been careless didn't matter. Robin was right, he'd gotten her into danger.

She didn't like this feeling of sick anger that was bleeding through her, but especially when it was directed at James. She'd never been mad at James before, had she? She'd known him literally her entire life, yet she couldn't think of another time they'd done anything more than bicker. But this was different. He could have gotten her killed. And she was brand new to this. What had he been thinking?

Shaking with anger, Gabriella carefully pulled on her clothes and brushed her teeth. Now the rest of the team was going to think she was useless at this job, and it was all because of James. They were going to think she was always scared and always needed to be rescued and that would be it for any respect she might get from them. And it wasn't like she could quit. She had to pay her bills.

By the time she was cleaned up and ready for breakfast, she wasn't hungry anymore. But she went out to the kitchen for some coffee anyway. There wasn't any brewed yet, Robin must not have been a coffee drinker. Gabriella pulled out a can of grocery store brand ground coffee and started up a batch. As it was beginning to brew, she heard voices coming from Robin's office.

"You need to get your head in the game!" she heard clearly through the door. "James, Gabriella could have been killed last night. What the hell were you playing at, not sealing the gateway?"

She heard James answer, but his voice was too quiet to hear clearly through the door. But it didn't matter, because Robin's response was even louder.

"'I could have sworn' isn't good enough!" he yelled. "You need to do it every single time. And if you think you did it, you need to redo it. This was an amateur mistake and I expect better from you."

Again, muffled sound from James. That sick feeling flared back up, but was tamped down by anger. He didn't seal something? That's how it got out? And what, she was just never supposed to find out unless she happened to be making coffee right here, right now?

The office door opened as Robin was saying, "We'll discuss this later. Team meeting in twenty minutes, you will be there and you will take responsibility for your mistakes."

James walked out of the office, face pale and expression haunted. He caught sight of Gabriella in the kitchen immediately.

"Gab-" he started helplessly.

No, she wasn't dealing with this right now. Her arm hurt, she was traumatized, and apparently it was all because he was careless on a case. So she just shook her head.

"Leave me alone," she said, then turned to pour her coffee.

***

The rest of the team was quiet as they all filed into the living room for the team meeting. The anger crackling off of Robin was apparently evident to everybody who hadn't been there this morning, since there was no joking or chatting as they filed in. Instead, Gabriella stayed in the chair while James sat miserably across the room on one of the sofas. Amelia and Madelyn sat down on the couch next to Gabriella's chair, both looking apprehensive as Robin glowered in the corner. Bradley came in last and sat next to James in the last open seat.

"Last night was unacceptable," Robin began in a low voice as they were all finally seated.

Gabriella couldn't help feeling a little grateful for his anger. It felt protective and fierce and after being so scared, the idea of someone protecting her felt good. Still, she felt a little bad that it was being directed at the whole group, and not just James.

"James was in charge, so obviously a lot of the blame falls on him and his own mistakes, but you all messed up last night," Robin continued. "You were supposed to do your jobs, you slacked on that, and Gabriella was hurt as a result. Instead of protecting her on her first job, you put her in even more danger."

Gabriella sneaked a glance around the room. Amelia looked like she was close to tears, while Madelyn looked down at her hands. James kept looking in Gabriella's direction, not daring to make eye contact. And Bradley just watched Robin with his expression closed.

"This is the best team in Massachusetts, according to the Foundation," Robin continued. "I take pride in that. And you should too. But if you're cutting corners on a case, you're clearly not taking any sort of pride in this work."

He stepped closer to James, who cringed just a little. "The creature you were fighting last night, the one that you were supposed to neutralize safely? That creature followed your teammate home and attacked her in her own bed. How is she supposed to trust any of you now?"

Now Gabriella could feel the eyes on her as she looked down at the shabby blue carpet. She was grateful for Robin's support, but he was laying it on a little thick, wasn't he?

"James."

James's head snapped up at Robin's call.

"You're suspended from fieldwork," Robin continued. "You'll be taking over Bradley's support role."

Bradley opened his mouth to protest, and Robin glared at him. "That's an order," he snapped.

Bradley closed his mouth and glared at Robin, who glared back. Then he turned to James. "You'll stay in headquarters, on support, until you've proven to me that you're capable of being a leader in the field. Do you understand?"

"Yes," James answered softly.

He looked crushed in a way Gabriella had never seen before. Not even during Gran's funeral or when his mother had been in the hospital years ago. It was like every trace of humor had left him.

Good, thought a nasty little part of her mind. It still horrified her that he would get her into this situation to, what, shave a few minutes off of an investigation? She honestly didn't know.

Robin finally looked away from James and at Bradley. "Bradley," he said. "God help me, but you're my second in command for the time being. You'll be taking over field cases when I'm not available."

Rather than be pleased at the promotion, Bradley looked like he'd swallowed a lemon. But he said nothing and just nodded as his gaze flicked toward Amelia and Madelyn for a split second.

"Don't fuck it up."

She could almost see the snarky response trying to force its way out of Bradley's mouth. Instead, he looked Robin in the eye and nodded.

Robin looked around the room at all of them. "Shape up," he warned. "Dismissed."

Bradley got up and immediately walked out of the room, disappearing down the stairs into the basement. Amelia shot a tearful glance at Gabriella, but hurried out of the room before saying anything. Madelyn's expression was cagey as she passed Gabriella and Gabriella quickly looked away.

She couldn't help stealing a glance at James, but he didn't look at her, just stared blankly at the floor. She wasn't about to start any conversations so instead, she got up and walked back toward the bedroom.

CHAPTER 12

THE BEDROOM WAS TOO small. It felt like the walls were slowly sliding toward her, like there wasn't enough air. Not enough room for the anger and confusion building in her body. So Gabriella walked back out after only a couple minutes of pacing.

To her relief, James was gone when she got back out into the living room. She could hear the sounds of muted voices coming from the basement as she walked down the steps and toward the front door. But she couldn't place who it was and frankly, didn't care. She needed to be alone right now to try and collect her thoughts.

The morning air was warmer than she'd expected, so she held the jacket in her good hand as she stepped out onto the front stairs and closed the door behind her. The neighborhood was quiet, which made sense. Mid morning, everyone was probably already at work or school. Trembling a little as she walked down the steps, Gabriella suddenly wished she was one of them. She didn't want to be here right now, stewing in rage. She wanted to be ten years old and riding that school bus that just passed by the end of the street, maybe on her way to summer camp. She wanted to know that monsters under the bed were just a scary story. And that her big cousin James would always be there for her.

She walked down to the cement walkway, where half-cooked flowers were trying their best to look cheerful. Nobody needed her right now, technically she wasn't even on duty. But what was she going to do, go home? Not a chance.

Instead, she stepped off the walkway and started walking along the side of the house. The side yard was smaller than the front, but there was plenty of space between Headquarters and the house next door. Someone had planted a scraggly line of bushes to designate the property line and Gabriella trailed her hand absently over it as she walked out back.

How could James do this? She couldn't get it to make sense in her mind, but it was the only explanation. There was a shadow person at the house. The same shadow person, the one James was sure he'd taken care of, was now in her apartment. The thing that wasn't supposed to be able to hurt her had torn her arm open almost to the bone. And the only way that could have happened was if James hadn't done his job correctly. She wanted to scream. She wanted to scream and cry until her voice was hoarse, to aim her pain and rage at James until he could see exactly how he'd betrayed her. It would have been so much less painful if it had been anyone else in the group. But it had to be her blood relative who'd gotten her hurt. The one she trusted the most.

The backyard was clearly better tended to than the sides of the house. As she walked in, she saw a small stone patio with a worn table and a couple of chairs. The backyard was lower than the back exit of the house, so there were stairs leading from the back porch down to the yard. Fang was stretched out on the bottom step, peacefully sleeping in the summer sun. Gabriella made her way over and sat down on the step above her.

"Hey, bud," she said softly as she ran a hand through her silky fur.

Fang opened one eye long enough to look at her, then shifted so that Gabriella and the sun could reach her soft belly. Gabriella stroked her fur, taking deep breaths as she tried to calm down.

She had a few options here. She could quit and find a different job. It wasn't like she'd signed a contract forcing her to stay with the Foundation, so she was free to go whenever she wanted to. She could leave this all behind and let them find someone else to take her spot. It wasn't like she was essential to the team, she was still in training after all. The safest option was to hand in her resignation and never speak to any of them again. Sure, Christmas would be awkward as hell for the rest of her life. But that would be the price she paid.

But she knew the truth. And she was pretty sure the Foundation didn't have memory-erasing technology. So she'd have to find a way to live in the world knowing full well what even her small area of it contained. And right now, even with the sun hot on her hair and the scent of zinnias in the air around her, she knew she couldn't do that. While she'd known there were strange things in the world well before starting with the Foundation, the sheer amount of confirmation she'd gotten over the past few weeks had changed her life.

So if she wasn't going to quit, could she transfer? Worcester wasn't that far, and she was pretty sure the Foundation had a branch there. If they were North County, who was taking care of South County? Hell, the training program was so dead set on her living in New Bedford. Maybe she could move to the coast.

That was the solution. A transfer. She'd go inside right now, go to Robin's office, and request that he transfer her to the next available position that wasn't in the North County branch.

As if on cue, Fang stood up, stretched, and walked away, tossing her a look over her shoulder. Gabriella stood up, wincing as the pain in her arm flared up. Then she started up the stairs.

The house was quiet as she opened the back door and stepped inside. From here, she could see the computer stations in the living room were empty. She closed the door behind herself, then walked into the dining room and knocked on Robin's closed door.

There was a second of silence, then she heard footsteps. The door opened and Robin glared out. Then he saw it was Gabriella and his cross expression melted into a smile.

"Gabriella," he said, suddenly cheerful. "Come in, come in."

He ushered her into the small office, closing the door behind them. It was crammed with bookshelves on either side of his desk, and she could see stacks of papers and boxes piled around the room. But Robin didn't seem fazed by the mess as he walked back behind his desk and motioned for her to sit down.

"I just wanted to tell you how happy I am that you've stuck with us," Robin started before Gabriella could say a word. "I know you've been through a lot, and many people would have quit or transferred after what happened yesterday. But you're clearly not just anybody. I've got big plans for you."

Gabriella's stomach sank as Robin smiled at her from across the desk. Who was she kidding? She wasn't going to transfer. So instead of saying exactly what she'd been rehearsing in the few minutes since she made her decision, she smiled and hoped it looked real.

***

All personnel are equipped with GPS whenever they leave their head-quarters for a mission. However, here at the Foundation, we believe in being prepared. Because of this, we require all of our members to learn alternative ways of finding their way in an unfamiliar place.

Gabriella closed her eyes for a second, then opened them as the screen faded out and a small hourglass appeared, spinning shakily in the center of her screen. She'd been trying to do this module for thirty minutes now and had gotten maybe fifteen minutes of actual learning done.

Click here to access an interactive sky map, set to your location. Confirm it is accurate, then consult the instructions on the next page.

Celestial navigation. Of course they were having her spend a glitchy hour plus learning how to navigate by the stars like some old-timey sailor. Just in case she ever needed to find her way home from Westminster and the highway ceased to exist. She clicked on the given link and the computer thought for a moment, making an unsettling grinding sound until it finally spit out a result.

NEW BEDFORD, MASSACHUSETTS 02741

Gabriella took a deep breath, trying not to scream. This was the equipment they had. And if this was what she needed to use in order to learn such important skills as how to navigate by starlight, so be it. She looked over the screen, looking for the link to change the location, but there didn't seem to be one available.

She was halfway out of her seat to ask James when she remembered she was furious with him right now. Between that and the glitchy computer, it surprised Gabriella to see that she was actually shaking with rage. She slowly sat back down, taking a deep breath and letting it out. She was at work and professionalism was key. Just like Mom had always told her when she was applying for jobs in high school and college.

It was a job. She could do this. So instead of pushing the computer onto the floor, she let out one last breath, then got up to ask Robin to help her.

CHAPTER 13

Robin made Gabriella take two days off from work to recover. She thought it was unnecessary when he said it, especially since he essentially kicked her out after a full day of work. She didn't love the idea of going back to her own apartment, but Robin had called for the mysterious Father McEnerney to come in and bless it. So that, along with the fact that all the protections the team had left on it last night were still in place, eased most of her concerns. She felt comfortable going there instead of going to her mother's, which would require her to confess everything that had happened.

So she took two days off and slept. When she wasn't sleeping, she was eating takeout, then crawling back into bed. Gabriella was actually proud of herself that she could sleep full nights in this apartment after everything that had happened. The lights stayed on and she'd stuffed about half of her belongings under the bed to fill up any space underneath. But she'd done it. And the enormous amount of sleep she got over the two days off made her feel fresh and ready to go when she got back to the headquarters a few days later.

As she walked into work, the first thing she saw was James sitting at one of the computers. He wore headphones and clearly didn't notice that she'd come in. "Alright, pulling up the specs now," he said to the person on the other end. "It looks like there's a cellar door over on the other end of the house. Do you see it on the property? They might have filled it in."

Gabriella didn't greet him when she walked up the stairs. As she'd left for work that morning, she'd thought maybe she was over it. Mistakes happened, after all. And he seemed genuinely upset when called out. But then, walking in here and seeing him working like nothing had happened, that infuriated her in a way she hadn't expected.

So instead of saying anything, she pointedly ignored him as he turned around to see who had come in. She walked into the kitchen and began searching through the pile of papers on the counter for her time card. Once she'd located it under a Chopsticks menu, she started filling it in for the week, pointedly keeping her head down and her hand steady as she wrote.

"Gabs," James said from the doorway a moment later.

She turned and glared at him. Now, seeing him up close, he looked like a mess, with red-rimmed eyes surrounded by dark circles.

"Gabs," he said again, "I'm so sorry."

She looked back down at her time card without a word. Why did he have to come in here? Didn't he see that she wanted to be left alone?

"I thought I did everything right, but I must have missed something," James continued.

"Yeah, apparently you did," she snapped.

He flinched as Gabriella looked up at him, her eyes stinging with tears now. "I don't understand why you'd cut corners," she said. "You knew it was my first case. Why wouldn't I be the one it went after?"

"I…"

She shook her head. "Save it," she muttered, then turned and walked out of the kitchen through the dining room doorway.

As she was passing through, she glanced into Robin's office. He was at the desk and had very clearly heard their entire exchange. "Gabriella!" he called out warmly. "Welcome back! Come on in!"

She walked into the office and he motioned her into a seat. "How are you feeling?" he asked.

"Um, better, thanks," she said, still vibrating with adrenaline after her confrontation with James.

"Good, good," Robin said. "I'm so glad to hear that."

She smiled back as he nodded, then glanced down at some papers on his desk.

"So Gabriella," he began. "Now that you're back, we're going to continue your training. You passed the first set of modules with flying colors and as soon as you're able, we want you back in fighting form exercising. But I'm going to be working with you on some self-defense training. Prevent anything like the other night happening again."

He laughed, but she couldn't quite bring herself to. Right, there had been a monster under her bed. Somehow being back here made that feel a little more real again.

"You'll be working with me on that," Robin continued. "It's nice out today, so I figure we'll start in the backyard. Do you have any assigned tasks this morning?"

"I think I'm on the cleaning roster to vacuum," Gabriella said.

Robin waved her off. "Don't worry about it, I'll have someone else do that."

She cringed inwardly. That was very nice of Robin, she figured. But whoever ended up with her chores was going to hate her if they didn't already. While everyone had been shaken at the meeting the other day, she'd noticed that nobody came outside to check on her afterward.

Not that she had wanted any company. But maybe they blamed her for the fact that James had gotten in trouble.

Robin clapped his hands together, jolting her out of her thoughts. "Alright then!" he said. "Go finish your time sheet and I'll meet you in the backyard. We'll be doing some basic knife work for now."

"Wait," Gabriella said. "What exactly is the weapons training going to be? I don't remember it from the handbook."

"The handbook is a little out of date," Robin explained. "Bradley is due for an update. But since our work is so varied here, we've adopted various kinds of weapons training as well. Knives, wooden stakes, occasional firearms. I have yet to send anyone into a situation where they need to carry a gun and I pray I'll never need to. But it's important to be able to protect yourself from anything, corporeal and not."

It had never occurred to her that she might have to carry a gun, and Gabriella really didn't like the feeling that accompanied this realization.

***

Despite the images that "knife work" conjured up, Gabriella spent surprisingly little time actually holding a blade during her training session with Robin. Instead, he mostly talked about the proper ways to hold it and defend herself from someone else who also happened to be holding a knife. By the end of their brief session, she could disarm him if he came at her very slowly, but that was it.

"And now you're dead," he said good-naturedly after he moved toward her faster than last time and she wasn't able to grasp his wrist and twist.

"I'm sorry," she said.

"Don't be, you're training," Robin said. "You're doing great, you just need to practice. How are you feeling?"

Her injured arm was burning a little, but she tried to ignore it. "Good," she said.

"Excellent," Robin said. "Alright, I noticed that you have a weights exercise routine scheduled today. How about you take some pressure off that arm and do an aerobic exercise instead?"

She nodded gratefully. "I'll do that."

"Perfect. I'm going to go back to the mountain of paperwork in my office. I'll see you for the afternoon meeting."

He walked past her and back into the house. Gabriella stood in the yard a moment longer, enjoying the cool breeze. Then she turned and reluctantly headed toward her workout.

***

When she got down to the basement, Madelyn was on the exercise bike with headphones on. She looked up at Gabriella as she walked in. "Oh, hi," Madelyn said, pulling off her headphones.

"Hi," Gabriella said uncertainly.

"How's your arm?"

"Um, fine."

"Good."

"How are you?"

Madelyn shrugged. "Alive."

Gabriella couldn't quite tell if that was a joke or not. So instead she just smiled and started walking toward the empty treadmill as Madelyn put her headphones back on.

Gabriella had forgotten her own headphones. She was so used to pop punk blaring if Madelyn and Amelia were working out together that she hadn't packed her headphones in days. She considered running upstairs to see if they were in her bag, but she was already so unmotivated that she knew going back out might actually kill her workout.

So instead she just silently climbed onto the treadmill and punched in her workout. Today it was a twenty-minute run, a good warm-up according to the cheery Foundation exercise instructions. From there it was weights and a machine she still wasn't entirely sure how to use. The treadmill's belt started moving, and she began to run, adjusting her speed until she was at a comfortable pace.

Gabriella tried to lose herself in the workout, in the repetitive pounding of her sneakers on the treadmill. But it wasn't working. After resisting for what felt like five minutes, she stole a glance at the screen timer.

Two minutes down, eighteen to go.

She could hear the tinny sound of music coming from Madelyn's headphones, but it wasn't clear enough to hear. She sped up, waiting for the ache in her calves to fade out. The first five minutes were always the worst part of a workout, right? Once the body was settled in and the muscles warmed up, it was so much better. She had to be there by now.

Two minutes and thirty seconds.

Gabriella started moving through her modules in her mind in an attempt to focus on anything other than the timer in front of her.

Vampires.

Vampires were real. There were different types, and each area had its own type. There was a nest in Westminster, but the Foundation hadn't given the go-ahead to take care of it. James didn't know why.

James.

James had nearly gotten her killed. She'd been so confused that night, but now it made perfect sense. It hadn't been something new that coincidentally got into her apartment. It was a monster that latched onto her on the case and made its move when she was vulnerable.

Three days later, the thought still made her shudder. It was suddenly too cold in the gym.

Five minutes. And her muscles didn't feel any better. That training guide was a crock of shit.

She looked up as Madelyn stood up and carefully walked over to the paper towels. She pulled one off, sprayed it, and went back to wipe down the exercise bike. As she moved, she softly touched the objects she passed, like she was bracing herself just the slightest bit in case she fell.

She didn't look at Gabriella as she cleaned off the exercise bike and threw out the paper towel. As she walked toward the door, Gabriella gave her a short wave. Madelyn nodded and waved back, but her small smile didn't reach her eyes. Then she turned and walked out the door.

Madelyn clearly hated her, Gabriella thought as a stitch began to spread through her side. But why? She hadn't gotten in trouble, at least not any more than everybody else. Was it because James got in trouble? Was she into James or something? Was everyone siding with him?

No, Madelyn had her own stuff going on. She probably didn't even think about Gabriella, let alone actively hate her. It was nothing.

Six minutes.

***

An hour later, Gabriella was freshly showered. She got dressed quickly in the pink bedroom, which now had a duffel bag sitting on the bed across from the one Gabriella had slept in last time. As she walked out, she heard voices coming from the living room.

"Bradley, you're better than this."

Robin's voice was sharp and tight and Gabriella winced in unexpected sympathy for Bradley. She walked forward a little hesitantly. The last thing she wanted right now was to get involved, but she had training materials in the living room that were already overdue.

"Robin, I've cut everything that I can possibly cut," Bradley said, apparently not affected by Robin's harsh tone. "I've budgeted us down to the penny, I've pushed off the bills that can be pushed off to pay the ones that aren't. I've reclaimed every single stash of petty cash we have in banks around the state. Today alone I've sent three requests to the Foundation for various parts of the budget to be expanded and I've got four more to send before I go home. I don't know what else you expect me to do here."

"Find something," Robin snapped. "This is your job, not mine. Find wherever this money leak is coming from and plug it."

"It's not a money leak," Bradley said in a long-suffering tone that made Gabriella realize this was an ongoing discussion. "Everything is accounted for. We just have too many expenses and not enough money to cover them."

"That's not possible," Robin said. "Fix it."

As she stepped closer, Gabriella could see Bradley's face. He looked puzzled for a second, then his face smoothed back into the unreadable expression she was getting more familiar with.

"Boss, you're asking me for the impossible."

"No, I'm asking you to do your job. Or else I'll find someone else who will."

Robin stood up and started walking away from Gabriella and toward his office. Bradley stood up too, picking up a pile of papers from the table. As she walked into the room, Gabriella could see her own papers beside his.

Bradley looked over at her and raised an eyebrow. "What do you want?"

He looked so disdainful of her that her explanation dried up in her throat. She managed to point to the papers and clear her throat. "Just need my papers," she said.

"Oh."

Bradley started to walk away, brushing past her as he walked down the hall toward the bedroom at the far end. Through the open door, she could see that half of it was set up almost as another office, with a computer on a neat desk and an office chair. Bradley turned around and gave her a hard look, then walked into the room and closed the door.

CHAPTER 14

GABRIELLA'S FIRST OVERNIGHT SHIFT was scheduled for the next night. Since she was still technically in training, she was only supposed to shadow the others and get used to being at the headquarters at night. But she was still nervous as she walked up the steps at seven o'clock that evening.

Fang greeted her at the door, purring as she weaved around Gabriella's legs. Gabriella leaned down and scratched behind her ears. "Hey, beautiful," she murmured.

Fang gave her one last rub and walked down into the basement. Gabriella watched her disappear into the darkness, then kicked off her shoes and walked upstairs.

"Hello?" she called as she reached the empty living room.

"Hang on!"

A second later, one of the bedroom doors opened and Amelia came down the hall. "Hi," she said. "It's you, me, and Madelyn on tonight."

Gabriella smiled at her and Amelia smiled back, but she didn't seem too enthusiastic. That warmth she'd shown the first couple of days Gabriella was working was nowhere to be seen.

"There aren't any cases tonight," Amelia continued. "So if you want to keep working on your modules, it's a good opportunity to do so. Madelyn is going to go get some dinner in a few, so let her know what you want."

"Oh, thanks."

Amelia nodded. "Yeah, no problem. I'll be on the comms all night, so let me know if you need anything. If any emergencies come up, we can go over how that works here."

She nodded one more time, then walked past Gabriella and into the kitchen. Gabriella watched as she poured a cup of coffee and added some milk. Before Gabriella could turn away, Amelia turned around and caught her looking.

"Help yourself to coffee," she said, motioning to the coffeemaker. "If the pot's empty, refill it. Seems like obvious common courtesy, but you'd be surprised how often people forget about those things."

If that was supposed to be a dig, she didn't show any sign of it on her face. Maybe Gabriella was being over-sensitive. "I will," she said.

"Good. I'll be in the back bedroom with the door open. Come in if you need me."

She walked away, leaving Gabriella standing awkwardly in the kitchen doorway. Not that Gabriella had been expecting it to be like a slumber party, but she hadn't expected to be left completely alone.

She went and poured a cup of coffee, relieved to see there was at least a full cup's worth left after she got hers. There was almond milk and two percent milk in the fridge, so she grabbed the almond milk and poured a little into her coffee before heading into the living room.

The computer she usually used was off, but the one beside it was still on. Maybe that one would be better. Gabriella sat down in front of it and pressed in her password, her hopes fading as the computer slowly whirred its way to the home screen. She took a sip of her coffee, wincing as the thick, bitter taste filled her mouth.

"Bradley made one more pot before he left."

Madelyn's voice made her jump. Barely avoiding sloshing her coffee onto her hands, she set the cup down and turned. Madelyn was standing behind her, leaning heavily on a cane. "He makes sludge," she continued. "I'd say don't tell him, but he doesn't give a shit. It works though, especially come, like, two o'clock when you're trying to stay awake."

She laughed a little, and Gabriella joined in. "I came out to ask what you want at McDonald's," Madelyn said.

A few minutes later, Gabriella managed to fish out her wallet out of her bag and pulled out some money for her order. For a second, she thought Madelyn was going to refuse it. But then she took the bills and folded them into her pocket.

"Thanks," Gabriella said as Madelyn turned to leave.

"No problem," Madelyn said. "I like getting out for a few minutes during the night shift. It gets boring. You're allowed to nap and watch TV and stuff, but you have to be on alert the whole time just in case."

Gabriella nodded, and Madelyn slipped out of the house. As the door closed behind her, Gabriella turned back to her module. Apparently, this week was all about survival strategies because now that the celestial navigation one was wrapped up, it was time to learn about shipwreck survival strategies. A little uncertain that this wasn't another New Bedford special, Gabriella clicked on the link and began to read.

***

Three hours later, the house was still silent. Occasionally Gabriella would hear Amelia talking to someone from the back room. The door was open and any time she looked over, Amelia would either be typing something or reading what appeared to be a Stephen King book. She had no idea where Madelyn was. The other woman had come back with their dinner orders, then disappeared to somewhere else in the house.

After finishing two modules, Gabriella's brain was fried. She stood up, stretched, and walked into the kitchen for a glass of water. As she was filling it, Amelia walked in.

"Hey," Amelia said, moving past her to get to the coffee.

"Hi," Gabriella said.

"How are the modules going?"

"Good."

"Good."

"Um, how's your night?"

Amelia shrugged. "Nothing exciting," she said. "There's a minor situation out in Palmer, but it's not in our area so I'm mostly observing and offering support."

"Would we ever go and help?" Gabriella asked.

"Only in a serious situation," Amelia said. "And it depends on the region. If you need backup, the night shift crew in the next region is your best bet. They can get there faster and they're more likely to be familiar with the area than someone from the other side of the state. Palmer has three other branches it could reach out to first. I'm just friends with the woman on site tonight, so we pass information along pretty regularly."

"That's cool."

She felt like such a little kid as she said it. That's cool? Amelia couldn't be more than three years older than her, but she still felt like a child right now.

"Yeah, you get to know people on the job. There are different trainings at the Foundation in Boston too, so you end up working with more than just your crew."

"Have you done any?"

"Yeah, I've done a bunch," Amelia said, taking a sip of her coffee. "Not that it'll get me anywhere with Robin."

She said it lightly, but there was an edge in her voice that made Gabriella flinch inwardly. But she was rescued from having to say anything when Amelia continued.

"For all the Foundation's flaws, they offer a lot of training that you really wouldn't be able to get anywhere else. So you can really specialize your team if that's what works best for your branch."

"Does Robin not want that?" Gabriella asked cautiously.

Amelia shrugged. "Who knows?" she said. "I just know I've done five conferences in five years and I've still never led a case in the field."

Gabriella couldn't tell if Amelia was looking for support here, but she wasn't sure what to say to that. She was still new, she had no idea what the office politics of the Foundation were.

"I'm going to go back to it," Amelia said. "Take a nap if you want to, it's a long night."

That sounded like a better idea than trying to tackle a third module right now. Gabriella nodded. "Thanks," she said. "I'll do that."

"Go anywhere but the pink bedroom. Madelyn's sleeping in there. She's not feeling good but she won't admit it."

Amelia's face was set in a grim smile that told Gabriella not to ask any questions. So instead, she nodded again. "I'll just stay out here," she said.

"Sounds good. I'll wake you up if anything comes up."

***

The rest of the night passed like boring clockwork. The phone didn't ring with a case once, and Gabriella spent most of the time alone in the living room area. She'd nap for half an hour, do a module, then repeat until the sun started coming up around five.

Even with the rest she'd managed to snatch, she still felt groggy and slightly nauseous at seven o'clock when the front door opened and Bradley walked in. He nodded to her as he took off his shoes and hung up his jacket.

"It's raining," he said instead of hello.

She glanced out the window. Between the curtains, she could see the rain coming steadily down outside. She hadn't even noticed.

Amelia and Madelyn were coming out of the bedrooms now. Amelia followed Bradley into the kitchen and Gabriella heard the two of them talking about the night. Madelyn sat down on the couch as though she were waiting to be dismissed.

"We always do a quick check-in with the morning person," she explained to Gabriella, who was sitting by the computer. "Obviously we leave notes too, but there has been some miscommunication in the past, so it's easiest to just do a quick meeting."

She was a little curious about what those miscommunications were, but wasn't about to bring the topic up. Not when Amelia, who had been so open and friendly those first few days, had spent the evening being a polite manager to her.

A few minutes later, the other two walked out of the kitchen. "Let's head out," Amelia said to Madelyn. "Bradley, are you all set?"

Bradley nodded. "McManus will be in in an hour, so I have just enough time to actually get some work done."

Amelia rolled her eyes. She looked like she wanted to say something, but then just turned to get her coat. "I'm on again tonight," she said. "Don't make this place too miserable while I'm gone."

Gabriella picked up her bag and started for the door. She was about to turn and say an awkward goodbye to Bradley, but he'd already gone back into the kitchen. So instead, she hurried down the stairs and slipped into her shoes, then stood awkwardly by the door.

Madelyn was slowly making her way toward the door. "Don't wait on me," she said to Gabriella. "Amelia's giving me a ride home. See you later."

Recognizing the dismissal for what it was, but too tired to over-analyze it, Gabriella followed her instructions and headed out the door.

CHAPTER 15

Gabriella was slightly out of breath as she left the gym and started walking upstairs. It had been a few days since she'd started working out again, and she was definitely feeling it in her achy legs and sore feet. But it encouraged her that the workouts themselves seemed to be getting easier.

"Gabriella!"

Only one person here was ever so cheerful when she walked into a room these days. Robin smiled at her from the kitchen as she reached the top of the stairs. "Finishing your workout?" he asked.

Had he missed the way she was sweating bullets and smelled like a gym sock? Gabriella nodded. "Yeah," she replied.

"Excellent. Glad you're getting back into the rhythm. Listen, let's have lunch outside."

She'd been planning to eat in front of the computer as she attempted to convince it yet again that she wasn't in New Bedford. But if everyone was taking their break outside, it might be nice to get out too. And maybe she could hope that the conversation wouldn't be completely awkward.

"Yeah, that sounds good," she said. "Um, I'll meet you all out there. I need to take a quick shower."

"Perfect!"

Robin seemed even more cheerful than usual today. Maybe it was the fact that she was overtired that was making it irritating rather than comforting. While her apartment was slowly starting to feel like home again, she'd woken up at least twice last night from overly bright nightmares where things slid out of the corners of the room and toward her bed. She was seriously considering moving at the end of her lease. And if this kept up, she might swallow the cost and break the lease before then.

Gabriella walked down the hall to the bathroom and knocked on the closed door. There was silence on the other end, so she opened it. She didn't hear any noise coming from the surrounding bedrooms either. Where were the others?

Maybe they were already outside. She'd shower quickly and head out. Even if James was going to be there, it wasn't like she could avoid him forever. They had managed to avoid each other almost entirely these days, to the point that she was pretty sure Robin was intentionally scheduling them on opposing shifts.

Maybe she should talk to him. She was only a month into this job and if she wasn't planning to leave it, they'd have to talk eventually. If she was honest with herself, she didn't see how she'd get back to fully trusting him again. But that didn't mean they couldn't patch things up at some point.

Gabriella stripped off her sweaty workout clothes and turned on the water. The shower clanged to life, and the water banged its way up the pipes until a weak spray came out of the showerhead. She put a hand underneath and hissed as the icy water hit her. Fine, it wasn't like her shower at home immediately warmed up either.

She took her time untangling her hair from its bun and laying out her towel. After a moment, she checked again. Still just as cold, even though she'd put the shower to its hottest setting.

If she was going to get outside soon like she said she would, she was going to have to suck it up and take a freezing cold shower, wasn't she? Groaning, Gabriella braced herself, then climbed under the water.

It took all of her willpower not to scream as the freezing water dripped down on her, running down her overheated back. It didn't even feel good on the parts of her body where she knew she was bright red and sweating, it was just unpleasant.

Gabriella showered as quickly as possible, teeth chattering as she scrubbed her limbs and face. She didn't even bother washing her hair, just giving it a quick rinse under the weak spray. Two minutes later, she shut off the water and shuddered. Was this another problem with the headquarters that they'd forgotten to mention to her? She quickly dried off and wrapped her towel tightly around herself.

She'd forgotten her clothes in the pink bedroom, but if no one was around, she didn't have to worry about anyone seeing her in a towel. So she walked the few steps down the hall toward the pink bedroom, teeth still chattering.

She walked into the bedroom and stopped in the doorway as she realized Madelyn was sitting on the far bed. She looked up as Gabriella walked in, and Gabriella could see she was trying not to smile.

"Forgot my clothes," Gabriella said, her face heating up despite the fact that the rest of her was ice cold.

"Happens to everyone."

Gabriella went to her bag and pulled out her work clothes, conscious of how little of her body the towel actually fully covered. Madelyn politely focused on whatever she was working on, keeping her eyes down as Gabriella gathered up everything she needed.

She'd been planning to get dressed in the room and head straight out to lunch, but she wasn't about to drop the towel in front of her coworker. So instead, she awkwardly left the room and went back into the bathroom. It was still cold in there, and she shivered. How was the cold shower chilling the entire room now? That didn't seem fair at all.

Five minutes later, Gabriella was dressed and hurrying outside. Madelyn hadn't seemed like she was in a hurry, so maybe the others hadn't gotten there yet. She grabbed her lunchbox out of the fridge and made her way to the back door. As she slid it open and started downstairs, she realized that the only person down there was Robin.

She tried not to be disappointed as she approached. How ungrateful could she be, getting disappointed that the only person who actually cared about her here wanted to have lunch with her? He turned and smiled at her and she tried to make sure her return smile was genuine. But she couldn't help the feeling of rejection as she joined him and took out her lunch.

***

"So how was your first full week?"

After a few minutes, Gabriella had relaxed enough to start enjoying Robin's company. He was kind. And genuinely interested in her. It was nice to talk to someone about this job who wasn't trying to end the conversation as quickly as possible.

"Good," Gabriella replied after swallowing a mouthful of food. "I'm glad I took the days off, but I think being in the routine is making it all feel a little more normal again."

"Good," Robin said. "It's a strange job, I know. But whatever your position, routine always makes things feel more secure."

He took a forkful of salad, spearing a tomato and wiping it in the Caesar dressing that was streaked on the inside of the bowl. "You're doing wonderfully," he said. "It's nice to see you settling into the job."

"Thanks."

"Don't worry about the others, they'll warm up to you."

Well, apparently she wasn't imagining things. He must've seen something on her face because he smiled ruefully. "I know you noticed," he said. "It's nothing personal, they're just a very tight-knit group. We all are. We look out for our own."

And she wasn't their own. James was. So no matter what had happened, they were going to be on his side.

"Give them some time," Robin said, popping the tomato in his mouth. "It'll be fine. Just keep doing your job well and they'll come around."

Great, now she had to work side by side with a bunch of people that not only gave her the cold shoulder, but were also so obvious about it that their boss noticed. Why was she so dead set on working here again?

"What's your favorite part so far?"

Robin's voice interrupted her spiraling thoughts. She looked up from her sandwich. "What?"

"Of the job. What's your favorite part of the job so far? I know your field experience has been less than ideal. But hopefully you've found something you enjoy."

"Oh, um, I guess the research? I've always loved local history, so that part has been really exciting."

"Is it?" Robin looked surprised. "I find it kind of boring myself so I force Bradley to do the research when we're working together. But it's nice to have someone here who enjoys it! Maybe we can expand your role in research a little more. What do you think?"

Working as a researcher? Gabriella thought for a second. That might be more her speed than working in the field with the others. "That would be great," she said. "Thanks!"

"Absolutely," Robin said. "You're a great addition to the team, Gabriella. I'm thrilled you're here so I want you to be happy to be here too."

She blushed and he smiled. "I mean it," he said. "You already bring a lot to the group."

Okay, now he was clearly flattering her. But she wasn't going to argue when her boss was complimenting her. So instead, she just smiled and started eating the last bite of her sandwich. Robin smiled back, then stood up.

"Well, I'm going to get back to work," he said as he gathered up his Tupperware. "Don't forget the team meeting at two. Then I think you and I should discuss some research possibilities."

He walked back into the house, leaving Gabriella sitting there with a smile. Maybe this was going to be fine after all.

CHAPTER 16

THE MEETING WAS EXCRUCIATING. While most of the team hadn't been openly hostile toward Gabriella since that terrible meeting a few weeks ago, she could feel the tension in the room as everybody filed in. James didn't look at her. This was possibly the first time he hadn't tried to catch her eye at least once. Instead, he walked in with Amelia and talked quietly with her for a few seconds, their voices too low to hear even from just the other couch. Neither of them even seemed to notice her.

Robin was right. They were clearly pissed. And if Amelia was mad, Madelyn probably was too. She'd just been being polite earlier.

And Bradley, but she assumed he was always angry. So that was nothing new.

She tried to focus on the meeting, but couldn't help stealing glances over at James as Robin began speaking. He was quiet, avoiding Robin's questions and not bringing up any topics of his own. The only person who raised their hand to bring up something that was not on Robin's agenda was Bradley, and he was ignored.

"So, tomorrow's case," Robin said after a detailed lecture about the importance of conserving gasoline while in the field. "Bradley, will you do the honors?"

Bradley had just dropped his hand and his face was sour as he stood up and pulled down the projector screen from above the fireplace. "Alright, so tomorrow's a ghost," he said, leaning over to start up the slide show from the computer beside him.

A map appeared briefly on the screen, then he clicked over to a photo of an old house. "We're staying local, this place is right over in Lancaster," Bradley continued. "Old farm house with a ton of history, at least some of it connected with murder. The activity the Foundation recorded on this site is intense, but standard. So we're going in with the usual approach. James and Madelyn will stay on base. Amelia and Gabriella, you'll be with me in the field. And Robin will be doing whatever it is Robin does."

"Signs your paychecks," Robin answered with a tight smile.

"It's stamped," Bradley retorted. "So we'll be taking a cleansing approach. Salt, holy water, the standards. Likely no need for weapons, the owner says it's alarming but not dangerous. No humans have been hurt, but it has a tendency to stir up the animals. Oh, right."

He made a face and clicked to the next slide, which showed a clip art red barn. "It's a farm. Activity is situated in both the house and the barn. So make sure you stretch beforehand."

He sat back down. Robin looked at him like he had expected something more, but then just stood up.

"I guess that's that," he said. "Amelia, you stay behind. But everyone else is free to go. Oh, Gabriella, you wait a moment. I need to talk to you after Amelia and I meet."

Amelia looked puzzled as she stood up and followed Robin to his office. Once again, James didn't even look at her as he walked silently out of the room behind Madelyn. Bradley picked up a textbook from beside his computer and headed down to the basement, leaving Gabriella standing awkwardly in the living room, waiting for her turn to meet with Robin.

The door was still open to Robin's office, and she suddenly heard a fierce murmur of conversation coming from inside. Robin's voice was too low to understand his words, but she could tell from the tone that he was furious. Not wanting to look like she was eavesdropping, Gabriella looked around the room for something to occupy herself. But all the textbooks, even *Introduction to Calculus*, were gone and it would look really fake if she tried to do anything else.

She got about halfway into the kitchen when the door opened all the way and Amelia hurried out. Her face was red and she was shaking as she walked through the living room. Gabriella opened her mouth to ask if Amelia was okay, but the other woman rushed past her and down the stairs toward the gym.

Watching her go, Gabriella suddenly felt the urge to join the others downstairs. She wanted to be part of the group. There didn't have to be an "us versus them" situation with Robin, right? And Amelia must have done something to get Robin riled up like that. He yelled sure, but he'd been so friendly and attentive to Gabriella and that seemed to be his normal personality. So maybe it was like what happened with James. Maybe she'd just been careless with something.

Gabriella turned as Robin walked out of his office. "Lots of history on this one!" he called cheerfully. "Come on in, we need to talk!"

He sounded fine, but maybe she was about to get yelled at too. Part of her almost hoped he would get mad at her. She didn't want to be bad at her job or disappoint Robin, but she didn't want to be the teacher's pet of the group either. But as she sat down in the seat in front of his desk, he sat down and smiled at her.

"So," he began. "I'm not sure how much you've heard about the Foundation's concern about strange energy readings in the region."

"Um, some," Gabriella said. "James mentioned it a while back."

"Did he explain what it was?"

She thought back, trying to remember from that conversation on her second day of work. "Something about trying to figure out what is causing them," she said slowly.

"We think it's lingering energy from some past event," Robin said. "But we don't know what that event would be, or how these houses with the strange readings are all connected. You said you're interested in local history, so I have an assignment for you."

Gabriella's heart sped up a little. A historical mystery? That was exactly the kind of thing she was interested in. "What kind of assignment?" she asked, trying not to sound overeager.

Robin slid a paper across the desk to her and she took it. It was a list of ten addresses, and most were either in town or right nearby. But a couple were miles away from their headquarters. "These are all the locations where the Foundation has tagged those energy readings," Robin said. "I want you to look through the history of each house on this list and see what connections you can find."

"Are you looking for any connections in particular?" she asked.

Robin shook his head, still smiling. "Nope," he said cheerfully. "That's going to be your job. Look into the history of each and note anything that jumps out at you. Or anything that might be a commonality between it and the others."

Her heart sank. Gabriella knew she should be grateful for the work, but she couldn't help thinking it sounded an awful lot like busywork. Was there really not a better way to find connections than having her look through four hundred years minimum of information for each house? "Do we have any books here that might have that information?" she asked.

Robin grimaced. "Not that I know of," he said. "You'll probably need to go to the library. How about you go and set up a research plan, then come back to me before you get started? I can help you get your hands on any books that might be trickier to get."

Okay, maybe it wasn't just busywork. Maybe this was actually important. She nodded and he smiled again. "Excellent," Robin said. "And don't forget your workout today."

Had she ever forgotten a workout? She'd literally told him when she was finished with her workout earlier. Was that supposed to be a dig at her since he was doing it with everyone else? But he was still cheerful as he stood back up and Gabriella followed. "Do you think you can have a list of books on my desk for the end of the day?" he asked as he led her to the door.

"Yeah, that's no problem," she said.

"Excellent. I knew I could count on you. This is something that the Foundation has been struggling with for a while. I think if you can solve the mystery, it would look very good for you with the higher-ups."

It would probably look good for Robin too, but that sounded mean even in her own head. "I'll work hard on it," she said instead.

He clapped her on the shoulder. "That's my girl."

He led her out, then closed the door. The living room was thankfully empty still, but she didn't feel the same urge to go downstairs with everybody else anymore. Instead, Gabriella pulled out a piece of printer paper and sat down at the messy dining room table. She pushed a pile of books and equipment aside, then set down her paper and fished a pen out of the same pile she'd just scattered. Putting the paper

Robin had given her on one side, she glanced over the list of addresses and turned back to the blank page.

Maybe she could start at the beginning? But the beginning of what? The current house on that particular piece of land? When the town had been settled by colonists? Time itself? Did he want her to just find the history as far back as possible and start reading until something showed up? This was clearly important if it kept coming up. So why hadn't anyone else started on it yet?

But that didn't matter, because now she was starting on it. So pushing aside the feeling of uncertainty and the nagging thought of busywork, Gabriella started thinking of potential starting points.

★★★

"Gabriella."

Gabriella looked up from her notes a little while later to see Bradley standing over her, glowering. "Hi Bradley," she said.

"We need to talk."

She put down her pen and sat up straight. "What's up?" she asked.

"I don't know what your problem is, but you need to stop treating James like this."

Her stomach twisted, but she just tried to keep her face calm as she looked up at the man looming over her. "Like what?" she asked.

"Like what happened at your apartment was his fault," Bradley replied.

She couldn't help the fact that her eyes darted toward Robin's closed office door. She wasn't sure if he was still in there or not. Bradley just looked at her as she turned to him.

"It was his fault," she said.

Bradley frowned even deeper. "No, it wasn't."

That anger that had settled down into a dull ache for a while now flared back up. "Look, I'm not saying he did it on purpose," Gabriella said. "But he messed up, and it ended up coming back on me. I think I'm allowed to be angry about that."

"Do you really think that's what happened?" Bradley asked.

"What do you mean?"

Of course that was what had happened. It was the most logical explanation. Bradley didn't even like James. Why would he ignore the fact that this was the most obvious possibility?

"I watched that case from the base, remember?" Bradley said. "I watched and listened to everything that happened. McMa - James - didn't cut any corners. He did exactly what he does every single time. What we were all trained to do."

"Then how did the spirit attach itself to me?" Gabriella demanded, her face hot. "How did it get into my house? How did it get under my bed? It was under. My. Bed."

"I don't know," Bradley admitted. "But I do know that it wasn't James."

Gabriella shook her head. "No," she said. "I don't know what you're trying to pull or cover up or what, but it's not going to work, so don't even try. I don't think he did it on purpose and I'm not going to, like, report him to the Foundation or whatever. He's my cousin and I love him. But he messed up on that case. And because of that, I got hurt. So yeah, I think I'm going to stay mad about it."

Her heart was pounding and she was grateful that she was sitting down for this instead of standing, because her knees would have definitely been shaking. She wanted to be the one to leave the confrontation, but if she stood up, she'd probably fall back down again.

Bradley looked at her for a long moment and she felt vaguely like a bug under a microscope. Then he sighed and shook his head. "Whatever," he said. "Believe what you're going to believe. I tried."

Before she could think of anything else to say to that, he walked out of the room. She heard a door close a little ways down the hall and turned back to her work. Were they really going to try to cover up what had happened to her? Was this the point they'd reached?

Whatever. She didn't know what Bradley's game was, but she'd just ignore it and do her work.

CHAPTER 17

The house looked like something out of a horror movie. Huge chunks of siding were falling off the outside walls, piling up in rotten heaps among the snarls of vines trailing along the side of the house. As they pulled up into the dirt driveway that wound through the massive, unmowed front yard, Gabriella noticed the front porch looked like it was about to slide right off. The peeling paint on the front created grotesque patterns across the walls and one of the top floor windows was boarded up.

"Please tell me this place is abandoned," Amelia muttered as they climbed out of the van and looked up at the building looming over them.

"No one has lived here since 2006," Bradley said. "The house and the thirty-five acres around it are owned by a family over in Acton and they want to sell it."

"But they can't," came James's voice across Bradley's speakerphone. "Because of the ghosts."

"Even in this market?" Amelia asked.

James laughed easily, and something in Gabriella's stomach clenched. He was the one that had hurt her, not the other way around. So why did she feel so uncomfortable right now, while the rest of the group readily accepted him?

"Alright, be extra careful inside," Bradley said, not acknowledging James or Amelia. "I'm not going to the hospital today."

Gabriella winced at this. He didn't need to look at her or acknowledge her for Gabriella to know it was a dig meant only for her. Nor did anyone say anything in response to his comment. Maybe Robin had been wrong, and they weren't ever going to warm back up to her after all.

Amelia started walking toward the front door. "Yeah," she said, as she pulled on the metal screen door and it came off in her hand. "Yeah, let's get this over with."

Still holding the screen door, she turned back to where Bradley was strapping the camera to his chest. "Alright, James, Madelyn," he was saying. "Do you have a visual?"

"Did Amelia just pull down a door with her bare hands?" James asked.

Amelia laughed. "See if you make fun of my coffee drinking habits again," she said, waving the rusted door threateningly.

"Put it down," Madelyn ordered over the speakerphone. "You're going to need a tetanus shot."

Amelia put the door down against the dingy storm window next to the now-empty doorway. Gabriella stepped up behind her, peeking into the dark doorway. Inside the house was even scarier than the outside. The electricity had obviously been off for years. As they opened the heavy front door, the movement stirred up a cloud of dust, stinging Gabriella's eyes. She coughed and waved it off.

"You alright?" Amelia asked quietly from beside her.

"What?" Gabriella jumped, surprised.

"Just making sure you're alright."

"Yeah, I'm fine, thanks."

Amelia nodded, then stepped past her into the dim kitchen. Gabriella followed and Bradley came in behind her. He left the door open, but the sunlight barely penetrated the room. In what little light filtered through the tattered curtains, Gabriella could see that the kitchen furniture was still sitting in the middle of the room. The table had the leaves unfolded and six chairs were neatly pushed in around it. Plates of different sizes sat at each spot and silverware was neatly arranged beside each one. In the center of the table stood a crystal vase holding a single flower. The crystal was tarnished almost to the point of being unrecognizable. The flower was desiccated.

"That's creepy," Amelia muttered.

"It looks like it hasn't been touched," Gabriella said. "Like they just left it."

Amelia nodded toward the living room beyond the kitchen. "Look at that though."

In the doorway, Gabriella could see that the living room furniture was covered in tarps. She stepped a little closer and peered inside. Every piece of furniture in there was covered or pushed to the sides of the room. The wooden floors looked original to the building and could have been beautiful, if not for the scuff marks and stains under a layer of dust.

That was exactly what she had expected to find when they came inside. Either emptiness or dust covers over everything. Signs that nobody had lived in this building in years.

She looked back at the table that looked like someone set it for dinner tonight. "Yeah," she agreed. "Yeah, that's creepy."

"What's creepy?" came James's voice over Bradley's phone again.

"It looks like we've got a dinner invite," Amelia said, stepping further into the room. "Bradley, come in a little closer so James can see it. The table is set for Sunday supper while the rest of the house looks like it hasn't been touched since the seventies."

"That fits the MO," Bradley said, walking over to the table. He picked up a fork and inspected it closely. "Family members have heard the sounds of people downstairs when they're upstairs."

"Wait," Gabriella said. "I thought nobody has lived here in years."

"They haven't," Bradley said with what she thought was an unnecessary lack of patience. "But they still have to maintain the property, don't they?"

"Plus, they own the property beside this one," Madelyn added over the phone. "It looks like some relatives run a brewery and farm stand about two miles from here."

"I could go for a beer right about now," James said.

There was a murmur of assent from Amelia and Madelyn. Bradley set the fork he'd been holding back where he found it. "Anyway," he said. "According to one owner, she was up there at one point and could hear and smell something cooking. Apparently one of the many murders that occurred here happened in the kitchen."

"Great," Amelia muttered.

"Alright, so what's the plan?" Madelyn asked.

"Let's ask Amelia that because Robin made a terrible decision putting me in charge tonight and we all know it," Bradley said, circling the table. "I haven't done any fieldwork beyond observations in months and I'm sure sexism had nothing to do with his decision."

"I've seen your pay stubs and you've seen mine, so I think I'm alright taking that responsibility," Amelia said. "Not like Robin's here to argue it. Again."

The look on Bradley's face made it clear that Gabriella was missing some context here. There were obviously conversations happening lately that she wasn't a part of. But instead of elaborating, Amelia just walked past the set table and into the living room.

"Alright, so this is where the Foundation said the apparitions appear the most, right?" she asked.

"Correct," Bradley replied.

"So I'm thinking this should be where we do the actual ritual and then bubble it out to the kitchen. Then we'll head out to the barn."

The barn was the part that Gabriella was dreading most. If the house was this creepy, she couldn't even start to imagine how bad the barn was going to be.

The moldy curtains and piles of garbage blocking several of the panes immediately dampened any sunlight that was streaming into the living room windows. It was a big room, and even in the dark, Gabriella could see even darker patches where other rooms branched off. There was a staircase on the far end of the room and Gabriella hoped they weren't planning to go upstairs for any of this.

"Can we get those windows open?" Amelia asked, looking up at where they all seemed to be glued shut with grime. "I can't reach over all of this stuff."

Gabriella looked up at them. Amelia was at least a few inches shorter than her and she was pretty sure she and Bradley were about the same height. She reached over a wrapped pile of garbage and tugged on the window.

"I think it's locked," she said, grunting as the window stayed exactly where it was.

After several tries at several windows, they had to admit defeat. "Okay, this is still doable," Amelia said. "That front door is still open, so there is an exit for the spirits if we can get them out."

Neither of the others spoke as they set up a wide ring of salt in the center of the room, carefully avoiding contact with any of the covered furniture or belongings. Once the circle was completed, Amelia and Bradley stepped inside it while Gabriella hesitated on the other side for a second. Then Bradley huffed a sigh of frustration, reached out, and pulled her in as well.

Amelia pulled out a small notebook and started reciting something in Latin. Gabriella couldn't catch every word, but she heard enough to know that it was a variation on an exorcism, similar to the ritual James had performed last time. She held a flashlight over the notebook, shifting occasionally to give Amelia a clear view of the text. Meanwhile, Bradley held a flashlight and rotated it around the room, intermittently illuminating every corner.

The whole room, previously empty, was now filled with faces. Every flash of the light revealed another distorted face watching them from the shadows. Some had grimaces spread unnaturally wide across their skulls, while others just stared blankly ahead. One made eye contact with Gabriella, who tried not to scream as it winked at her and melted away.

"Are you seeing that?" she whispered to Bradley, her heart racing.

"Yes."

She waited for him to elaborate, but he just continued to cast his flashlight over figure after figure. Amelia's voice kept going, loud and confident, and eventually, the smirks slid into silent screams. The figures started melting together as the beam moved faster and faster over them.

Then, with a flash of fire lighting up the corner of the room, they were gone and Amelia was silent. They all stayed where they were for a few seconds, the only sound in the room their uneven breathing in the darkness.

"Update?" James asked over the speakerphone. "I can't see shit."

"I think it worked," Amelia said.

"I think so," Gabriella agreed.

"Alright, let's finish this off so we can get out to the barn," Bradley said. "Amelia, you stay in the salt for a few minutes and keep watch. Gabriella, you get the holy water. I have the incense. Let's not cut any corners."

Gabriella cringed and hoped it was too dark to see it. Amelia said nothing, but she could hear Madelyn's voice on the speakerphone. "Bradley," she muttered.

Bradley ignored her. "Come on," he said to Gabriella. "Every corner of the first floor. Then we should check on the second floor. If there's just a few wispies left, the owners don't care. It might be shocking, but they were mostly concerned about our friends in the corners."

"The report here says there has been no activity reported on the second floor," James said. "Did the Foundation request energy readings?"

"Not that I've been told," Bradley said. "They don't seem overly concerned about that whole thing these days, but I'll take them and send them over anyway."

He motioned for Gabriella to join him. She followed silently, splashing holy water into each corner as Bradley waved incense. He didn't say anything to her as the smoke curled through the house, and she was grateful for it.

"Upstairs," he said, making his way over to the stairs.

She hesitated and he stopped. "What?" he asked.

"Nothing."

Bradley looked like he wanted to say something, but then just turned and headed up the stairs. "Walk carefully," he called down to her. "Flashlight won't show everything."

Upstairs they stepped into a long, narrow hallway. "Do you have a visual?" James asked over the speakerphone.

"No, it's completely dark," Bradley said. "Hang on."

He shined the flashlight down the hall, carefully sweeping through the corners and the two doorways on each side. "I'm not seeing anything," he said.

"I don't like this," James said. "Are you armed?"

Gabriella felt her lunch rising back up her throat. But she could almost hear Bradley roll his eyes. "Yeah, I walked in completely unprepared. Fuck off, McManus."

"Shut up and answer the question."

"Yes, I have a knife."

"Gabriella?"

She jumped. "Yes."

"Good."

Gabriella half-expected James to say something more to her, but he didn't. Instead, she heard him say "I've got visuals" before the line clicked.

Bradley pulled out a small device and turned it on. It began blinking in the darkness. "What's that?" Gabriella asked.

"EMF," Bradley replied, scanning the area. "You should have reached that module."

What she should have done was just not open her mouth, apparently. Instead of answering, she waited with the holy water in one hand and a flashlight in the other, following him as he ran the device through all the darkened rooms of this floor. Thankfully the atmosphere up here was less terrifying than downstairs. There were signs of human life in the empty bedrooms and that demonic feeling was gone.

"Alright," he said. "I've got what I need. Come on."

They made their way carefully down the stairs. "Barn's next," Bradley said as they got back to Amelia.

"Any murders in there?" Amelia asked.

"Plenty, don't worry," James said. "Brad, you got the details?"

"If you never call me that again," Bradley replied.

There was a pause, then Bradley sighed. "Yeah, there were three murders in that barn over the course of fifty years. All back in the late nineteenth and early twentieth century."

"Any connection?" Amelia asked.

"The same family's owned the property since 1840, so yeah."

Amelia made a face at him that Gabriella could see in the dim light. "Got ourselves a little New England Conjuring House, don't we?" James asked.

"I think the actual Conjuring House is the New England Conjuring House, but sure," Madelyn said.

Madelyn and James laughed while Bradley narrowed his eyes. Gabriella felt that feeling in the pit of her stomach again. Maybe this had been a mistake.

Removing malicious spirits from an old barn full of sharp farming equipment should have been terrifying enough to distract her, but Gabriella couldn't stop feeling like she was on the outside of the group, even more than she had been before. Amelia and Madelyn were being polite enough to her, but Bradley didn't even bother to hide his disdain and James hadn't said a word to her outside of the weapon confirmation.

So she was basically going through the motions as the same scene unfolded. Same demonic figures popping up in the corners, same bloody illusions in the flickering light of Bradley's flashlight. This time, instead of smirking visages, there were flashes of murder, like snapshots that burned themselves into her retinas.

And then, just as quickly, it was over. The barn was silent except for the wind slapping some broken shingles.

Half an hour later, they were back in the car. Bradley had insisted on being meticulous about wrapping up the case, to the point where Gabriella was pretty sure the overkill was being directed at her. He'd inspected every corner of the barn twice, ran an energy sensor over it at least three times, taken EMF readings and EVPs, and then went back to the house and did the same thing in every room all over again. Finally, he'd declared himself satisfied and they went back to the van.

"Robin's not back," James said over the speakerphone as Amelia pulled the van out of the farmhouse's driveway. "So I guess we just debrief each other."

"What is Robin's deal lately?" Amelia said, untying her ponytail and shaking her head. She pulled onto the main road and sped up the van. "He's being a wicked dick."

"It's weird," Madelyn said over the phone. "He's so mad, like, all the time."

"He's chewed me out twice for the smallest things," Amelia said. "Yesterday he said I wasn't doing my entire workouts. Which is ridiculous, I do extra workouts, you all know that. But he pulls me into his office and basically says that if something happens on a case because I can't pull my own weight, it's on me."

"He's being ridiculous," Bradley muttered. "It's like he's looking for things to get mad about and if he doesn't find them, he'll make them up."

He didn't look at Gabriella, but once again, the implication was obvious. She sat silently in the middle seat, next to the equipment. Robin hadn't been mean to her at all. If anything, he had been overly friendly lately. He'd been warm and welcoming, like a favorite teacher back in high school might be. Maybe he wasn't quite that way toward the others, but it was weird that there would be this much of a discrepancy between how he treated them versus how he treated her.

"Has something changed?" Madelyn asked over the speakerphone as Amelia stopped at an empty red light between two fields.

"Not really," Amelia said. "Even whatever he thinks happened with James doesn't add up with this new shit he's pulling. Madelyn got tossed off a building and he didn't start vanishing for days at a time and yelling at everyone."

Why was Gabriella even still working here? They all clearly resented her for this. That wasn't going to change, and none of it was her fault. She hadn't asked for the thing to be under her bed or for Robin to act as her mentor. She hadn't asked for any of it, but apparently they weren't going to let her forget that they blamed her.

Something must've shown on her face as Bradley turned around to search through the bag beside her in the middle seat of the van. "Don't even start," he muttered.

Something flashed in her chest, hot and sudden. "Start what?" she demanded.

He looked at her for another second, then just rolled his eyes.

"Brad," James said over the speakerphone.

"Call me that again and I lead you into traffic on your next field mission," Bradley muttered.

"I'd have to get back in the field first."

James sounded more bitter than Gabriella had ever heard him. Over the past couple weeks he'd avoided her, but kept some semblance of humor with the others. But even with the distortion of the speakerphone, it sounded like a mask had slipped, just for a second.

"He's got me doing my own job, plus yours," Bradley said. "He better get you back into the field soon."

"Look," Amelia said, her eyes still glued to the road, "Let's just agree that Robin's being a jackass, we don't know why, and we're all tired of it."

The others chimed in their agreement, but Gabriella still sat awkwardly silent in the backseat. It didn't feel right to start shit-talking Robin too, not after everything he'd done for her. Amelia either didn't notice or didn't care, but Bradley's eyes flicked up to the rearview mirror to glance back at her. Avoiding eye contact, she looked out the window toward the dark fields passing by as they drove back to headquarters.

CHAPTER 18

Gabriella had just finished her workout and now the chocolate banana smoothie she'd left in the fridge was calling to her. So after getting changed, she headed out to the kitchen with her mind on some of the mundane history research she'd been doing for Robin earlier in the morning.

As she walked into the room, James was already in there, pouring a cup of coffee. He glanced up and smiled when she came in. Then he realized who was there and his smile faded.

"Oh, hey Gabs," he said, turning back to his coffee.

"Hey," she said softly.

He picked up his mug, then set it back down and turned to her. "Look," he said. "Gabs, I'm sorry. I don't know what I messed up that night. I've been tearing it apart over and over, watching the tapes, and trying to figure out where I went wrong. I can't find it, but apparently, I did something, and you got hurt. And I'm so sorry about that."

Gabriella's appetite evaporated as she stood in the doorway, looking at her cousin. She missed him. And after weeks of walking on eggshells around each other, she missed the casual closeness they'd always had before now.

James kept watching her, clearly waiting for a response. Gabriella wanted to accept his apology, so maybe it was time to move past her anger and just do it. She wanted so badly to just get back to normal. He hadn't meant to hurt her and he'd paid the price for his mistake, right? So why was she still hanging onto it weeks later? Her injury was healing and she only had occasional pain from it. Maybe it was time to move on.

Screw it, she needed to get over it.

She felt the corners of her mouth turn up just a little. But as she opened her mouth to tell him she accepted his apology, she heard Robin call in from his office.

"Gabriella," he said. "Can you come here for a moment? It's urgent."

James picked up his mug, then slipped past her and out of the room. She turned in time to see him round the corner, then looked back over toward Robin's doorway. He was waiting at his desk, an expectant look on his face. Now that the moment had thoroughly escaped her, she started walking toward Robin.

"What's going on?" she asked, pausing just inside his doorway.

"It's about your research," Robin said. "The library just called, they have the books you were looking for."

That was what was so urgent? Something twisted uneasily in her chest as Robin looked at her. But Gabriella just smiled and nodded, keeping the urge to scream buried in her chest.

"Great," she said, resisting the urge to turn around and chase after James. "That's great, thanks."

"You should go pick those up before they close today," Robin added, still smiling.

There was a knock at the door frame behind her and Bradley poked his head in. "Sorry to interrupt," he said. "Robin, can I speak to you in private?"

Robin motioned toward her, and she moved to let Bradley in and walk away. But before she could get out the door, he held out a hand to stop her. "It's just Gabriella," he said. "There's nothing secret among team members."

Bradley looked first at her, and then at Robin with his face set in what looked like a deliberately neutral expression. "Fine," he said. "Which bill would you like me to put off this week, boss? The overdue electric bill or the overdue internet bill?"

"And why exactly are they both overdue?" Robin asked, his temper clearly controlled under his calm tone.

"Because we don't have the money for both?" Bradley replied, his own voice now showing signs of strain under its cool professionalism.

Robin's smooth expression fell for a second and for that split second, Gabriella thought she could see a strange sort of rage come over his features. Then his mask slid back into place and he glanced over at her, then back at Bradley.

"Let me look at the accounts when we're done here," Robin said. "We'll find the money in there somewhere."

Bradley nodded. His gaze flicked from Robin to Gabriella. Then he turned and walked out of the room.

Robin shook his head and smiled warmly at Gabriella, that blank fury now gone from his expression entirely. "Some of your teammates," he said with a patronizing smile.

He pulled his laptop toward him and opened it up. "Alright, you should go pick those books up," he said.

Recognizing the dismissal for what it was, Gabriella nodded and slipped out of the room.

***

A few hours later, Gabriella and Bradley were both working at computers in the living room, each determinedly avoiding looking at the other. She would have rather done her research in one of the bedrooms, but Amelia and Madelyn were napping in one right now while the others had already been claimed by James and Bradley, who were scheduled overnight. She knew James would gladly let her use his room, but he didn't want to ask him that, not right after she'd accidentally avoided accepting his apology.

So now she was seated at one end of the room while Bradley sat at the other end. Occasionally he'd huff out a sigh and glare at his computer, but beyond that, there was silence except for the clicking of keys.

The books she'd brought back from the library were excruciatingly boring histories of the Montachusett region, where most of the energy readings came from. They were so delicate that she was worried pages were going to fall out as she worked on cross-referencing details with the websites she'd found. She wasn't quite sure what the end result of this research was going to be, but Robin had been talking about how even if she didn't find connections between the houses yet, an in-depth history of the region could come in useful with some of the hauntings they regularly investigated. So she might as well gather as much information as she could.

After about an hour of squinting at the tiny text in the rapidly fading sunlight and losing track of unnumbered pages, she was rescued by the sound of Robin walking into the room. "We've got a case," he said.

Bradley looked up and scowled. "Emergency?" he asked. "There was nothing on the docket tonight."

"Urgent," Robin said. "Direct call to Leominster State Forest. It should be simple though, we don't need the whole crew."

Bradley was already switching programs to pull up the Foundation's information, but paused at Robin's words. He raised an eyebrow at that. "No?"

"No, I'll take Gabriella with me and we can take care of it."

Gabriella's head shot up and she stared at him. "What?"

"No need to be nervous, you've got this," Robin said. "It's a simple one, think of it as a practice session. You'll do great. Come on, get your shoes on."

"No pre-brief?" Bradley asked.

Robin shook his head as Gabriella stood up and picked up her bag from where it sat by her feet. "No, it's a simple one," he said. "We'll be back before dinner. I'll buy us pizza. Come on, Gabriella!"

Gabriella caught Bradley's eye for just a second, then Robin hurried her toward the door.

***

She'd expected Robin to give her all the information on the case as they drove there. But he was quiet as they got into his car, a small gray sedan. He stayed silent as they pulled out of the neighborhood and headed toward downtown. Instead of offering any explanation, he fiddled with the radio. He'd pause for a second on some pop song or sports chat, then hurry along to the next thing.

After about ten minutes of this, Gabriella cleared her throat. Robin glanced over at her as he slowed down and stopped for a red light.

"Thanks for coming along," Robin said. "Not that I don't trust your teammates, but I think this is an excellent opportunity for you to really show your stuff."

"What is it?" Gabriella asked.

Wasn't he supposed to explain all of this before they went into the field? Even if it was just the two of them on a simple task, she was uneasy going into the dark woods with no details about what they'd be doing there.

"Simple haunting," Robin said, eyes going back to the road as the light turned green. "It's out in the State Forest a little ways so we'll have to do some walking."

Great. Gabriella hadn't worn a jacket and it was already dark, so this was going to be a fun time. She tried to swallow her irritation and focus on the task at hand.

"Okay," she said, looking out the window as they passed an empty-looking bank and a packed bar.

Robin didn't say anything else as he drove. Gabriella waited a moment for him to continue, but it quickly became obvious he would explain nothing else before they got to their destination. Wasn't that protocol though? Not doing a briefing was odd enough, but she didn't know anything about the case beyond the fact that there was apparently a ghost in the woods. And now she was also under-prepared for it. If Robin was so big on protocol these days, then what was this all about?

He knows what he's doing, she assured herself, glancing over at Robin as he drove. He looked over and gave her a warm smile. "Put whatever you want on the radio," he said. "I'm fine with anything. Oh, and check the backseat for me if you can see it. Make sure the holy water and salt are ready to go."

Gabriella turned in her seat and saw a bag of salt and a vial of holy water sitting in the backseat. The sight of them made this whole situation feel a little less weird. Maybe it was a test of some sort? Was that the Foundation's style?

"I can't tell you how happy I am that you joined the team," Robin said as they moved away from the lights of downtown and onto a more wooded street. "You've really brought a lot to this job. And I think with a little more time, you could really be a great leader."

He thought she could be a leader? Seriously? Gabriella felt like she could barely be a follower right now. But her skepticism melted somewhat at the warm smile on Robin's face as he drove. "I know it's only been a few weeks, but I can see it," he continued. "You've got an eye for this job and I think that's something that'll bring a lot to the Foundation."

"Thanks," Gabriella said, blushing a little.

She still wanted to know more details, but his calm demeanor was easing her own worries now. Robin knew what he was doing. So she'd just follow his lead on this one.

CHAPTER 19

About fifteen minutes later, Robin pulled the car into the small gravel parking lot at the edge of Leominster State Forest. This wasn't one of the major park entrances that Gabriella was used to, the ones that had a well-lit gravel parking lot and other people. But she could see that it led to the beginning of some of the State Forest hiking trails.

The lot was tiny and otherwise empty, but there were signs barely visible in the darkness showing the way onto the paths. A single streetlight illuminated a small patch of dirt lot as Robin turned off the engine and they got out of the car.

Gabriella opened the back door and grabbed her bag out of the seat. She glanced inside to confirm everything was there, then zipped it up and slung it over her shoulder. Holy water, salt, and a blade. Her standard gear, but he hadn't told her if she needed anything else.

Robin pulled out a bigger bag and slid it onto his back. "Alright, let's head out," he said as he passed her a flashlight.

"Do I need anything else?" Gabriella asked, glancing back into the car where an assortment of equipment was scattered on his back floor.

She turned on the flashlight and it flickered a couple times before settling down into a watery beam of light. It illuminated the shadowy brush along the sides of the lot. What kind of ghost were they going to be dealing with here? Robin said it was a simple haunting, so hopefully it was just some house in the middle of the woods. They'd take care of it, go back to the house, and then she could try to get a moment alone with James so that they could talk.

"Nope," Robin answered her cheerfully, glancing up at the moon above them. "Alright, follow me!"

He led her to the path entrance closest to his car. It was wide and neatly swept, almost surprisingly so. But as they got a few steps further into the woods, the vines were already creeping out from the sides of the dirt path, brushing against Gabriella's sneakers as she walked. She shone her flashlight down on them and caught a familiar reddish-green hue on some of them.

Great, poison ivy. Why hadn't Robin given her any information before they left the headquarters? At the very least, he could have given her time to get some long pants on if he knew they were going into the woods.

"So what exactly is this?" she asked again as they began to walk steadily down the thickly lined trail. "It doesn't have anything to do with the strange energy readings, does it? I've been looking into the state forest for connections, but nothing has jumped out at me yet. One of the houses is located within the borders of the forest, but there doesn't seem to be anything linking to the others."

"Standard haunting, like I said before," Robin said as he deftly stepped over some branches on the path ahead of her. "It's a little ways up here, just off the trail in a small stone foundation. You'll know it when you see it, trust me. But it's the usual. Screams, moans, shadows that nobody can explain."

"But nothing physical?" she asked. "Any other manifestations? Who reported it?"

In the weak moonlight coming through the heavy coating of leaves above them, she could see Robin turn and smile indulgently at her. "You're so good at this job," he said. "I meant what I said in the car. Though, I have to admit, when James said he wanted to bring on his cousin, I wasn't so sure about it. Nothing personal to either of you, of course. It's just that bringing on family members rarely works out in any job, let alone a job that requires so much training and trust."

"Thanks?" she said, wondering if she should feel insulted. And why was he bringing up family and trust right now? If she didn't know better, she'd think Robin was needling her about James. But why would he do that? He already knew she was hurt by what happened. And that her relationship with James was probably never going to be the same. He didn't need to rub any salt in that wound.

Robin laughed as he turned back around, but it sounded a little brittle. Gabriella didn't blame him if he was nervous. It was dark and they'd already lost sight of the tiny parking lot. The path was getting a little rougher already, and the half-buried stones she kept hitting were starting to hurt the soles of her feet as they pressed through her thin sneakers.

Suddenly Robin sped up his pace, walking hurriedly through the branches growing over the path. Gabriella matched his pace, pushing aside the branches slapping her face as she tried to catch up. The path had brought them so far into the woods already that the trees completely swallowed the few street lights visible behind them, leaving them moving only by the light of the moon and their weak flashlight beams.

A stick cracked under her foot and she stumbled a little, catching herself as Robin slowed and turned around. "Keep up," Robin called, voice still cheerful, but a little more strained now. "The ghosts aren't going to wait around for us."

She hadn't been on many cases yet, but Gabriella couldn't help the uneasy feeling forming in her gut as she skipped over another small branch and sped up a little to catch up with Robin. Did anyone except Bradley even know they were out here? They should really have someone working with them at base, just in case. Sure, Robin probably knew exactly what he was doing. So it wasn't like they needed the team here. But what happened if Robin got hurt? She had no idea what she was going to do if something like that happened. Not that it was likely to happen, Robin was a professional.

But she knew all too well that accidents happened.

"Should we call and let them know our location?" she asked Robin, who was pushing the branches aside as the path grew thinner in front of them. "Before we lose service in the woods?"

"No, no, they know."

A branch snapped back in her face and Gabriella caught it in her hand before it cracked her tooth. Something was wrong here. She was new, but she wasn't so clueless that she couldn't pick up the signs. But why would Robin bring her out here like this? It wasn't some random person. This was her boss. The one whose job it was to keep her alive. The idea of him trying to hurt her was ridiculous.

Maybe she was just being paranoid. She didn't want to be rude to Robin, or make him think she didn't trust him. So she was just going to keep her mouth shut and get her nerves under control so that they could do the job and be done. Then she'd work on whatever was wrong with her that made her so wary.

Then Robin stopped. Nothing on the path had changed, he just stopped so suddenly that Gabriella almost walked into him. She jerked to a stop and nearly stumbled over the bramble now overgrowing the path. Robin didn't seem to notice anything as he stood with his back to her, gazing into the darkness ahead.

"Robin?" she asked.

"The Foundation won't help us," Robin said, still facing away from Gabriella.

"What?"

"I tried to get them to increase our budget and cover all the bills," he continued. "But they kept telling me I was doing fine as it was. That the team was doing well and there was no extra money to pad our budget. This was bullshit, I know what kinds of endowments they have. They've got more money than Harvard does. But they rejected all of my grant applications. We're just too good at our job."

He laughed, but it was sharp like broken glass and something in it made the hairs on Gabriella's neck stand up. This was wrong. Something was so so wrong right now. She glanced back in the direction they'd come from, but the darkness had swallowed the path.

"I thought if something went wrong, they'd realize they have to give us more money," Robin was saying, his voice a monotone as he continued to avoid looking at her. "But then Madelyn got hurt. She was so badly hurt, Gabriella. We didn't think she'd make it. But she pulled through and we were all so relieved. And when they did nothing beyond paying her medical bills, I knew that it wasn't enough. All I had done was just hope and hope that maybe they'd realize we needed more help. But all they offered was another position. I asked for more, but they said the position was all they could give. Take it or leave it. So I took it. And I took whoever happened to come along to fill it. And if something were to happen to them on the job, something worse than what happened to Madelyn, then the Foundation would have to realize we don't have the resources we need in order to keep everyone in our region safe."

Gabriella knew she should run. Even as her mind denied everything that was happening in front of her, the rest of her being was screaming at her to get out of here. But she couldn't. Something kept her rooted to this spot as Robin spoke.

What did he mean, something worse than Madelyn?

"R-Robin?" Gabriella managed to choke out.

"Nothing short of someone dying on the job would get us what we need."

There it was. There everything was. In that second, as Robin looked away from her and Gabriella tried not to cry, it all just fell into place. Like the information was dropped directly into her brain. That's all she was. She wasn't a teammate, she was a tool. She was here to serve a purpose and then be discarded.

She was here to die.

She should run. But just like that night in the apartment, when that thing followed her home from the case, she had frozen in place.

Wait, had it followed her home? Or had it been there already, waiting for her?

Robin finally turned around and in the dim light of her flashlight beam, she could see what looked like genuine anguish in his eyes. They were red-rimmed, maybe even shining with tears? But then her eyes dropped to the blade glinting in his hand.

"Gabriella," Robin said, shaking his head "I'm so sorry."

CHAPTER 20

THE KNIFE GLINTED IN the moonlight, the blade lethally sharp in Robin's grip.

"It's nothing personal," Robin said, his voice shuddering as he took a step toward her. "It overpowered you on the case, Gabriella. You were brave, you fought as long as you could. But it got you because we didn't have a way to get help in time."

Gabriella tried to say something, anything, to get him to stop. But all that came out when she tried to speak was a small choking sound.

"You shouldn't have survived the first time," he continued. "You got home and it should have killed you. A tragic mistake that could have been avoided."

The blade in his hand was less important for a split second as his words sank in. "You did that?"

"It would have been perfect," Robin continued, and she was horrified to see he was almost in tears. "The new girl, not quite fully trained, was followed home and killed after her first mission. It wasn't the same entity, but close enough that no one would know. But you managed to get out."

Bradley had been right, she realized as her horror grew. James had done nothing wrong. It had all been a setup. She wanted to scream at Robin, despite her terror right now. Scream at him for hurting her, for manipulating her, for what he'd done to James. What he'd convinced her to do to James. For isolating her from all the others.

But there was no time for that. She had to get out of here. Did he have a gun? She tried to shove aside her terror and remember if she saw him pack one back at the car. She didn't think so. Besides, a gunshot wound would be suspicious if he was setting it up to look like she died on a case. A ghost wouldn't shoot her, even the most dangerous one. So if he was going to make it a ghost or anything else that wasn't human, he couldn't kill her that way.

So maybe she had a chance.

Robin was still looking at her, and she could see tears swimming in his eyes. Something about them unnerved her more than anything else that she'd seen from him yet. But maybe, if he truly didn't want to do this, she had a chance to stop him.

"Robin," she said around the lump in her throat. "You don't have to do this."

"Yes, I do," he said. "I'm sorry Gabriella, but it has to be done. If we don't get more resources, we can't protect this region. And the only way we're going to get what we need is if we show them we can't do it in the conditions they give us. So we have to show them. And the most tragic result is the only one that they'll listen to. It's the only way."

He looked down at the knife in his hand, and it was as if a spell had broken. Gabriella's body could move again. Before she'd thought anything through, she bolted off the path and into the trees, the branches scratching at her face in the dark. She was still clutching her flashlight as she ran, stumbling over stumps and branches that were tucked within the leaves crunching under her feet.

She could hear Robin coming after her, not far behind. Gabriella flipped off the flashlight and the comforting beam of light vanished, leaving only the light of the moon just barely illuminating the woods ahead of her through the heavy leaf covering above.

"Gabriella," Robin called, his voice carrying clearly in the quiet night air. "Gabriella, it doesn't have to be like this! Just come back. It's for the greater good, I promise. You'll be a hero!"

She shoved through another spray of branches, zigzagging her way through the trees. Her footsteps felt unnaturally loud, like they were leading Robin straight to her, no matter how fast she ran. She flinched as a branch caught her in the eye and her foot landed in a cold puddle of something, but she didn't stop moving.

Just keep running, she thought. This is why you run on that god-forsaken treadmill every day. Breathe in, breathe out. Just keep going and you'll stay alive.

Robin and his words gradually seemed to fall behind her, but she didn't slow down. She ran steadily, shoving branches away from her face, no thoughts in her head now except survival. Breathe in, breathe out, stay alive.

Then there was silence. After listening to it for a few minutes, Gabriella slowed her pace. There was a stitch growing in her side as she slowed down to a walk, gingerly stepping through the dead leaves. She tried to keep her footsteps and heavy breathing as silent as possible.

It had been a setup. Everything from bringing her on board to separating her from James and the rest of the group. It had all been grooming her to be...

To be what, a sacrifice? What the hell was this? The budget was too tight, so she had to die? Couldn't Robin moonlight as an Uber driver or something like everyone else? Why did she have to get stabbed so that they could balance the books?

She ducked under a particularly dense-looking bush and crouched low on the ground, wincing as the mud seeped into her pant legs. The air was wet and cold on her bare arms and her teeth chattered as she caught her breath. She couldn't hear anything out there now. Robin must have lost her trail.

Gabriella pulled out her phone, saying a silent prayer as she did so. It was still on and the signal was weak, but there. She quickly dialed and held the phone up to her ear as it rang on the other end.

One...

Two...

Three...

Come on, she thought. James will answer even if he's mad. Right? If he didn't answer, maybe one of the others would?

Then the sound of the phone answering. "Gabs?" James answered, sounding hesitant.

"James," she whispered, eyes darting around in the dark for any sign of Robin. "I need help. I'm so sorry I didn't believe you."

"Gabs, what's going on?" James demanded.

"It was a setup," she continued, tears pricking her eyes. "Robin threatened to kill me. He's going to kill me."

She heard a sharp breath on the other end of the line. "Where are you?"

"Leominster State Forest. Somewhere, I'm not sure where."

She heard him set down his phone and her heart sank. She should have believed him, he'd help her if she had trusted him. He didn't have any reason to trust her now.

But then she heard the clicking of a keyboard and realized he'd put her on speakerphone. "Okay," he said. "I've got your location. It's okay. I'm leaving now, I'm going to meet you. If you can start walking west, you'll reach the road in about a mile and a half. I want you to get there and wait for me."

"You believe me?" she whispered, almost unable to get it out.

"Of course," he said simply. "I can't get a handle on Robin's location, he must have shut off his phone. You go. Stay on the line if you can."

She looked at her phone battery icon. Three percent that dropped to two as she watched. "My phone is going to die."

"Can you remember how to get to the road?" James asked.

"Go west. Keep walking west."

"And you're good with finding west?"

She considered it for a second. "I have my compass on my phone," she said.

"And if that dies? Will you be okay?"

Gabriella glanced up at the sky. It was pretty hidden, but there were enough gaps that she could see the stars. They looked identical to what she'd seen on that map on the computer.

Celestial navigation. It was going to come in useful after all.

"I think so," she said. "I can see the stars now."

He huffed a laugh, then got serious again. "Hurry," he said. "Just find the road and then I'll find you."

She carefully pulled herself out from under the bush, glancing in every direction for Robin before she moved. The woods were still silent, but that didn't mean he wasn't there, watching and waiting for her.

She flipped open the compass app. It shone on the screen for a moment, then her phone shut off before she could read it. It's fine, Gabriella thought to herself. You don't need it. You can find your way.

She walked a few feet over to where there was a break in the leaf cover, then looked up at the sky. She took a second to acclimate herself, grateful that the stars wouldn't be any different here than they would be in New Bedford. She craned her neck to get a better view, and after a moment, she could see Orion. And with that, she knew which way to go.

Ignoring the blood running sluggishly from cuts on her face and the squish of cold mud in her shoes, she started walking west. It was slow, quiet work as she carefully calculated every step.

She was cold, tired, and so confused and hurt. Thinking was harder than it had been before, her thoughts scattering as quickly as they formed. She'd trusted Robin. He was her teacher, her mentor. And somehow she hadn't noticed that he wanted to kill her. How could she have been so wrong? What the hell was wrong with her?

She walked for what felt like hours, but couldn't have been more than twenty minutes. This forest wasn't that big. It was a local recreation point, she was probably passing crushed beer cans and crumpled chip bags with every step. Gabriella had grown up around here and occasionally hiked with her cousins, but never at night and never in this area. Right now it all felt deep, overgrown, and weirdly ancient.

There were alien sightings in these woods, weren't there? And a Bigfoot? If she was going to run into a Bigfoot, it would probably be tonight, wouldn't it? Fuck everything about this night.

Focus, Gabriella told herself, looking back up at the stars to confirm she was going the right way.

Still no sign of Robin. She wanted to take out her flashlight to guide her way, but that would be a dead giveaway to her location, wouldn't it? And she had to hide her location because her boss had tried to murder her. Robin had tried to kill her. It was sinking in a little more now. Robin. Had tried to kill her.

A few minutes later, Gabriella could see the dark pavement of the road ahead. By now her legs were like lead, but just seeing it gave her an unexpected burst of strength. She ran, glancing behind her one more time to make sure she wasn't being followed.

As she reached the road, she glanced in either direction. Both ways were dark and silent. James had told her to reach the road and wait for him there, he'd find her wherever she was. Her phone was long dead, possibly not even in her pocket anymore. But she'd found the road and now he'd find her.

How had Robin not found her by now? She was so exposed here by the side of the road. A large *No Hunting* sign hung over her head and she almost laughed out loud at the irony. But if she laughed, she knew she was going to cry. And then she'd never stop crying.

She was crying right now.

That's when the headlights appeared up ahead. Her heart soared, then crashed. Maybe it was James. Or maybe it was a random stranger passing through.

Or maybe it was Robin and he was going to kill her this time.

She backed up into the brush, ducking behind a tree as the car pulled closer. Peeking out from behind the branches, she realized it was a van. It slowed down as it approached her location and with a flood of relief, she saw James behind the wheel. Madelyn sat next to him while Bradley and Amelia were in the back. James stopped the car and opened the door.

"Gabs?" he called.

She bolted out from behind the tree and threw her arms around him.

CHAPTER 21

"I'M SORRY, I'M SO sorry," Gabriella sobbed, gripping James's rough jacket as she buried her face in it.

He held her tightly in the driver's side doorway, shushing her as she cried. She couldn't even bring herself to be embarrassed about falling apart like this in front of the rest of the team as she tried to choke out what had happened. But she couldn't stop shaking and every time she was close to calming down, that feeling of being alone and doomed in the woods came right back.

"It's okay," James whispered. "It's okay, I'm just so glad you're okay."

She reluctantly let go and glanced down the street. The woods and the road behind her were silent and dark, but that didn't mean Robin wasn't on his way. "We need to leave," she said. "I don't know where he is. I lost him in the woods and maybe he's still in there, or he went back for the car or a gun or something, I just don't know."

The van's slide door slid open and Amelia poked her head out. "Get in," she ordered, beckoning Gabriella back.

Gabriella didn't need to be told twice. She ducked into the car and pulled the door shut behind her, nearly tumbling into Amelia, who climbed into the backseat, leaving her in the middle with Bradley.

"Now what?" Bradley said, glancing out the window as James started driving.

"We need to go to the Foundation," James said. "This is obviously not cleared with them. I checked the logs, they never called in a case over here and he never reported that he and Gabbie were going out on this one."

"This is insane," Madelyn muttered. "Guys, it's Robin, it's not some random person. It's our boss."

"Our boss who's been acting completely out of character for months," Amelia said. "And what, do you think Gabriella is lying about it?"

"Of course not," Madelyn said, with a guilty look back at Gabriella. "Sorry, I didn't mean to...it's just..."

"He's been so fixated on the budget," Bradley said, still looking out the window beside him. "He's been chewing my ass out about it for months."

He let out a long-suffering sigh. "When I said we shouldn't be so good at our jobs and maybe they'd give us more money, this wasn't what I fucking meant."

"We're going to need to stop for gas soon," James said. "But we should just go straight to the Foundation's headquarters. It's like an hour drive, but we can't go back to headquarters or any of our homes. I have no idea where Robin went, we weren't able to locate his phone or get in touch with him. So we need to bring in the upper levels to figure out what happens next."

Headlights cut through the darkness behind them as they dipped over a small hill. As the beams illuminated the car, Gabriella looked around at the group around her. They all looked exhausted, almost haggard. And there was definitely a degree of irritation in the car that was directed at her.

But they'd come for her when she needed them. They all had.

"Thank you," she said, emotion tightening her throat. "For coming to get me. I'm so sorry I didn't believe you before."

The other three didn't say anything, but she caught James's eye in the mirror and he smiled at her. "We're a team, Gabs," he said. "And it's not like you're the first to trust the wrong person. One time Brad-"

He was cut off by the growl of an engine behind them. As she turned to look, Gabriella realized in horror that the headlights she'd seen before were blocked now as the car pulled up inches away from the van.

"It's Robin," Madelyn said, turning around in her seat. "What the hell is he doing?"

In the red glow of the taillights, far too close, she could see Robin through the windshield of the car behind them. He pulled out his phone as she watched.

"He's calling me," James said as his phone vibrated on its dashboard stand.

"Don't answer," Bradley snapped.

The phone kept ringing, then Gabriella's head snapped forward as Robin rammed the car from behind. She heard Madelyn make a pained noise as the van lurched ahead. She turned around again and made eye contact with Robin, who held up his phone and nodded at her.

"Answer it," she said, turning to face forward again. "He's going to drive us off the road."

James reluctantly hit the answer button on his phone. They were silent for a second as the phone connected.

"Pull over," Robin said.

"Robin, I don't know what's going on, but this has gone too far," James replied. "We're going to the Foundation."

"They won't help you," Robin spit through the phone. "They wouldn't help me keep you safe, why would they help you now?"

"Robin, this isn't keeping us all safe, you fucking asshole," Bradley spit from the back seat. "You tried to kill one of the team."

"She's not part of the team," Robin snapped, and again, they were all shoved forward as he rammed the car from behind. "She was a temporary asset that would get us what we needed. It would have been better this way. The Foundation would have realized we need more support and they would have given it to us. We'd have everything we need to keep our area safe, but you're going to ruin that!"

"I'm not going to let you just murder my cousin," James said, voice sharp with disbelief. "Are you serious?"

He hit the gas and the van jerked forward, gradually inching away from Robin's car. The rest of the road was dark ahead of them, but the headlights cast shadows that showed they were completely alone out here. Gabriella was pretty sure they were coming up on some form of civilization, but if Robin kept ramming the van, they might not get there in time.

"Robin, do you even hear yourself?" Madelyn demanded. "What the hell happened to you? You're talking about murder to get a few extra dollars in the budget. Do you realize how messed up that is?"

"You know what's messed up?" Robin demanded, his voice crackling on the phone slightly as the engine groaned under the force of James speeding up the van. "Trying to keep the entire northern half of the county safe from every supernatural threat Monsterland could possibly throw at us! And on a shoestring budget that makes us choose between paying the electric and the internet. To fight goddamn demons! We're not doing this. Either stop the car and let Gabriella out or I'm going to drive you off the road. An entire dead team will work just as well as a tragic accident in the woods."

"He's insane," Amelia breathed as the car creaked its way up a steep hill. "Can you go any faster?"

"I'm trying," James said tightly. "I swear to God I'm going as fast as I can."

Behind them, Gabriella could see the headlights glow bright just behind them for a second, then whip out beside them, crossing into the opposite lane.

"What the fuck is he doing?" James demanded.

He clearly tried to speed up, but the old van wasn't having it. Robin weaved into the lane and he jerked away, narrowly missing the guard rail as Robin pushed him further toward the edge of the road.

"Speed up, speed up!" Gabriella nearly screamed.

"I'm trying!"

She watched in horror as Robin reared back into the opposite lane and tried again. He made contact, sideswiping the van just enough that James lost control. Sparks flew outside the window as it scraped against the guardrail. Gabriella was tossed into Bradley, who grunted in pain as her elbow pushed into his chest. She tried to apologize, but the words stuck in her throat.

Robin pulled back again and Gabriella knew with terrifying certainty that this third time was going to be the one that sent them through the guardrail and into the ravine. And that she was helpless to do anything about it as they reached the crest of the hill. Looking at Bradley beside her, she could see the same fear echoed on his face.

Then there were new lights coming from in front of them. Bright lights and the thunderous roar of a heavy engine moving quickly over the hill. And it happened too quickly for her to process. The tractor-trailer crested the hill coming in the other direction as Robin was pulling back into the opposite lane to land that final blow. And then the crunch of metal meeting far more metal as the tractor-trailer slammed directly into Robin's car, a head-on collision that sent him back down the hill as the truck driver tried desperately to stop.

This time everybody screamed as James whipped the van into a dirt shoulder that came up quickly on their right. He stopped the car and hopped out before anybody else, rushing across the road and toward the smoking, crushed wreck of what had been Robin's car. It had rolled partway down the hill and stopped there, lodged in the guardrail on the other side of the road.

The others slowly got out of the van. Gabriella's whole body shook as she opened the sliding door and stepped out onto the pavement. Across the street from them, the weeping truck driver was saying over and over that he didn't understand what just happened. That he'd tried to stop and what was that guy doing in this lane, were they racing?

As Gabriella watched, James stepped up to the wreck and looked into what remained of the driver's side of Robin's car. Without a word, he staggered back and vomited over the guardrail. Gabriella went to follow him, but Madelyn held her back.

"Don't," she said. "There's no good coming out of seeing that. He's dead."

CHAPTER 22

IT WAS SEVERAL HOURS later when the van finally pulled into the driveway at headquarters. Once the police had arrived on the scene, they'd questioned everybody about what had happened. The interrogation was a bit of a blur to Gabriella even before it was over, with one disbelieving officer asking if she was really sure the victim was trying to murder her. Could she maybe have misunderstood the situation?

At one point, she'd seen Bradley step aside with one of the cops. From then on, the investigation had taken a different tone, with the two officers losing a bit of their swagger. The fear on the younger one's face made Gabriella wonder how entrenched the Foundation was with local communities. But the implications of that made her want to lie down and never get up.

But eventually, it was over. The paramedics treated the truck driver for shock. James, despite his own haunted expression and shaking limbs, had made sure they checked Gabriella too. She was worried they'd make her go to the hospital, but the paramedic had listened to her with kind eyes and agreed that she could go get some rest.

Now they staggered up to the front door of Headquarters. Amelia unlocked it and the group stepped inside, silently kicking off their shoes and making their way to the living room. Nobody had planned to meet there. But Gabriella realized they were all going there anyway.

James sat down on the couch and ran his hands down his face. "What...the...fuck," he mumbled.

Bradley had his own face buried in his hands as he sat on a chair along the wall. "I need to call the Foundation."

"Do they even have someone on this late?" Amelia asked.

"They better."

Bradley stood up and fished in his pocket, coming up empty-handed. "I think I lost my phone."

Gabriella felt her gaze pulled toward the darkness behind Robin's open office door. The others were clearly looking there too. Was there another official business phone in the building? The idea of ever going into Robin's office made her nauseous and she imagined the others felt similarly.

Amelia took out her phone and handed it to Bradley. "Use mine," she said, then leaned her head back against the back of the couch and closed her eyes.

Bradley disappeared down the hall as he waited for the Foundation to pick up his call. Gabriella looked at the others. Amelia seemed to already be asleep. James was staring at the floor. Only Madelyn made eye contact.

"How are you?" Gabriella asked.

"Sore."

"Do you need anything?"

Madelyn shook her head. "I'm fine," she said. "How are you doing?"

Gabriella paused, a little unsure how to answer that. "Alive," she finally said.

Madelyn laughed and Gabriella joined in, but she knew they both sounded frayed and shaky. Their laughter trailed off into silence. Then she looked over at James, who didn't seem to be aware of anything that was happening around him at that moment. He was just looking blankly at the floor in front of him.

"How are you?" Gabriella asked hesitantly.

This seemed to jerk him out of his daze. "Wha-I'm okay." He said. "You okay, Gabs?"

She wanted to pour it all out right then, how sorry she was for not believing him, for falling for Robin's manipulations. For thinking he'd hurt her. But before she could say anything, Bradley walked back into the room. He nudged Amelia, who opened her eyes and looked up at him.

"They're going to send someone out tomorrow morning," he said, handing back her phone. "Apparently our captain getting himself killed in a murderous plot isn't urgent enough to get someone here tonight."

"Are we sure he's gone?"

Gabriella wasn't aware she had that fear until the words were out of her mouth. Her eyes went back to the darkened office and her stomach churned in newly sparked fear. "What if he comes back?" she asked.

"He won't."

James's voice was muffled by his hand over his face. They all turned to look at him, but he didn't look at anyone.

"Trust me," he said. "Robin's dead."

Amelia slid her hand into his and he gripped it tightly. Gabriella wanted to stuff the words back in her mouth and judging by the look he gave her, Bradley would have been willing to help her do so.

"Sorry," she mumbled. "I didn't mean to-"

"It's fine," James said.

The room fell silent again. Amelia closed her eyes while Bradley stood by the window, staring outside into the night. James continued to sit motionless in his chair and Madelyn gave Gabriella a sympathetic look. She smiled and Gabriella smiled back, feeling a little less alone.

Then she yawned and leaned her head against the chair, closing her eyes for just a moment...

"Hey, Gabriella."

Amelia's voice and the sensation of someone gently shaking her pulled Gabriella back to consciousness. She opened her eyes.

"We're all heading to bed," Amelia said. "I didn't want to leave you out here alone. Are you coming?"

"Is there a bed left?" Gabriella asked, rubbing her eyes.

"The grey room has one," Amelia replied.

"I'll be in in a sec."

Amelia walked away and Gabriella took a deep breath. She let it out slowly, trying to send away the images of tonight that were slowly seeping into her mind.

Robin had tried to murder her. He'd hunted her in the woods. But now she was alive and he was dead. She'd won.

And she might never be able to reconcile the image of the tearful killer with the kind smile he'd given her that first day. She'd probably never know how much of his warmth was manipulation and how much of it was genuine.

Gabriella stood up and stretched before she could go further down that train of thought. She needed to get some sleep. Tomorrow they'd all start processing what happened tonight.

She made her way over to the gray bedroom and stepped inside. It was dark, but she could see James was asleep in the far bed.

"Goodnight," she said softly as she quickly pulled on her shorts and tee-shirt and climbed into the other bed.

"Goodnight," he mumbled.

Gabriella pulled the covers up and hoped that the nightmares wouldn't come just yet.

***

The Foundation representative that showed up at Headquarters the next morning was friendly enough, but something about him put Gabriella's teeth on edge. He was a little too calm and polished about the situation. As if team leaders regularly tried to murder their new hires and then killed themselves by driving headlong into a tractor-trailer. There seemed to be a procedure in place for this as well, and she wasn't sure how she felt about that.

But for now, they were all sitting in the living room as he sat in an upholstered chair and explained what was going to happen next.

"So we will get you a new captain, don't you worry," he said, taking a sip from the coffee Bradley had offered him.

He winced, then tried to hide the fact that he'd winced and set the coffee aside. "But it might take a while to get everything organized," he continued. "And to be honest, we're a little short-staffed right now. So in the meantime, James, you'll be in charge. You've got seniority here."

James kept his face neutral, but Gabriella had known him long enough to know that look. He would rather chew glass than be in charge. But he nodded. "I accept that," he said.

Bradley rolled his eyes and Amelia quirked a slight smile. Madelyn made eye contact with Gabriella and the corner of her mouth turned up just a little. Gabriella smiled back, then turned back to the rep.

"So James, we'll be in touch later in the week to get you oriented. There are some extra training modules you'll need to do as well. I know it's a very sudden promotion, so we'll be flexible about the time frame in which they need to get done."

James nodded, face still politely neutral. "Appreciated."

"Do you have any other questions for me?" the rep asked.

James shrugged, then glanced around at the others. Nobody spoke. "No, I think we're good," he said.

"Alright then," the rep said, standing up and leaving the coffee behind. "I won't take any more of your time. Good luck, and let us know if you need anything. We'll be in touch, both about the training and Robin's permanent replacement."

He walked out with James a minute later. When James returned, he looked at the group gathered in the living room.

"I don't think it's a secret that I don't want this job," he said. "But I'll do my best with it. And I promise to keep you all safe. And not murder anybody."

He turned to Bradley. "You interact with the Foundation all the time," James said. "There's not a chance they're getting back to us with any of those things, is there?"

"Absolutely not," Bradley responded. "We'll hear from them again sometime in June when it's time to balance the budget."

"I'll look forward to it. Amelia, obviously you're second in command."

Gabriella saw the smile light up Amelia's face before it settled into something more professional. She nodded and James smiled and nodded back.

He fell onto the couch beside Gabriella and smiled. "I'm glad you're here," he said to her. "Not just that you weren't murdered, but that you want to be on the team."

"I'm so sorry I didn't believe you," she said.

The guilt had been eating at her all morning, ever since she woke up to the slanting light coming into the bedroom. When the reality of everything had crashed down on her. She should have known. She'd always trusted James, so why was she so quick to dismiss him when everything pointed to him being right? Everything except Robin's story.

James slung an arm over her shoulder and pulled her in for a hug. "It's okay," he said. "I know how it is. And I get it. Hopefully you can trust me from here on out."

Now there were tears in her eyes. "I do trust you," she said, trying to keep her voice even.

He squeezed her, then let her go. "Alright," he said. "Who wants breakfast? My treat."

"Not saying no to that," Amelia said.

As they stood up, there was the sound of a bell ringing from the computer. Bradley went over and opened the message.

"Report of some creature out on the edge of town," he said, reading the screen as he spoke. "Someone saw it leaving Walmart this morning and there's been enough sightings in the past hour that the Foundation wants us out there investigating."

"What, like right now?" James said.

"The voice of a leader," Bradley snarked.

"Yeah, well, this leader wants breakfast."

Bradley glanced at the screen again. "Yeah, right now."

James sighed dramatically. "Alright. Here's the plan. First, we check out the Walmart cryptid. Then we go to Denny's. Come on, let's go."

He headed for the door as the others got up to follow. Gabriella stood a little slower, looking around the room for a second. She'd nearly died last night. And now she was right back here. And she couldn't help the excitement that was bubbling up inside her at the thought of what this creature they were heading out to check on might be.

She nodded softly to herself, then stood up and joined the rest of the team as they walked out the door.

END OF BOOK 1

Want a Bonus Epilogue?

Sign up for my email list over at BookFunnel and receive a FREE exclusive bonus epilogue to North County Paranormal Unit!

You'll also receive alerts for new books, sales, and exciting bonus content!

Sign up here:

North County Paranormal Unit #2: Jarvis Street

Read on for a sample chapter of North County Paranormal Unit #2: Jarvis Street, now available at your favorite retailers!

Jarvis Street: Chapter 1

It was hot in the living room at Headquarters. A heatwave had been smothering Central Massachusetts for a couple weeks now, and even this early in the morning, the air in Leominster felt heavy and thick. The front windows above the worn couch were closed, but it would have been even worse to have them open to let in the steamy air. It was just after seven in the morning and the weather report said it was already in the high eighties and climbing. The small living room felt sticky, both the old furniture and the Foundation command center overheated and more cramped than ever.

James had stripped down to just shorts and a tank top before he sat down at the small bank of computers to do his work, but his fingers were slick with sweat as he typed and he could feel a bead dripping down his back. He'd worked the overnight shift with his cousin Gabriella last night and he'd sent her home an hour early to get some sleep. The day shift were all supposed to be in in about thirty minutes, so he was drinking his coffee and trying to make the slightest dent in the mountain of tasks he needed to do before they arrived and the day added twenty more things to his pile.

The air conditioner in the window in front of him was humming, but the sound was sickly and there wasn't much cold air coming out of it. He wanted to get up and check on it, but there were so many other things vying for his attention right now and the rest of the team would be in shortly. So instead, he settled for the weak stream of slightly chilled air as he tried to parse out what he was supposed to be reading on this monthly budget overview.

It had been a month since The Foundation for Paranormal Studies, New England's top paranormal investigation and eradication society, had named him interim captain of their North Worcester County branch. He'd been the second in command at North County for years with no desire to be in charge. But then their former captain, Robin, had attempted to murder Gabriella in a convoluted scheme to convince the Foundation that they needed more resources if they were going to take care of the region properly. Robin had been killed in the ensuing fight and the Foundation had promised to get a new captain in as soon as possible.

Looking at the numbers in front of them, James had to admit they did need more resources. Murdering his cousin wasn't the way to get that money, but from the parts he could understand, he could easily see that things were going to get rough this month. He hadn't even had time to dig into it and approve anything yet, not that he really knew what he was doing with that. The program he had to use was slow and glitchy on their outdated computers and, without any instructions to translate with, the codes looked like nonsense. He'd been trying to get this done in between tasks for two days now and he had gotten nowhere with it.

Though, to be honest, James didn't know what he was doing with most of his tasks right now. The promised training materials and replacement captain the Foundation had said were on their way had yet to materialize. The captain thing didn't surprise him. He had a feeling he was in the spot for the long term. However, he'd expected them to set him up with some training manuals at the very least. James knew what to do in the field and he knew his way around a curse or a cryptid. But he had no idea how the computer system worked and it had taken him and the team's logistics coordinator, Bradley, a week to realize that he not only had a new email address, but all of his previous passwords and accounts had been canceled.

Bradley found a way to blame James, of course. But there was no way James could have known. Had the Foundation emailed him about it, then deleted his email account? They would do that, wouldn't they?

The numbers were blurring on the screen in front of him and James shook his head. He had napped for about an hour last night while things were slow, but that was the only sleep he was going to get all day and he knew it. Oh well, he'd power through with coffee and energy drinks, then sleep afterward. He'd done it plenty in college and even though he was now over a decade out of school, he could still do it. At least until things settled down.

God, this job sucked. It had only been a month, but he was floundering and things were falling through the cracks. He didn't know how to write a schedule in the system, he didn't know how to communicate with staff and the home office through official channels, and he was completely overdue on the performance reviews that Robin had apparently been working on before he died in a blaze of...something.

James rubbed his eyes, trying to get both the sleep and the memory of Robin's mangled corpse out of them. Christ, he just needed to focus. Did they all really make so little money? And was there any way to shave off anything at all in the budget? He was supposed to meet with Bradley to go over this soon, but he didn't even know where to begin with it. What did half of these words even mean?

Looking at the flickering screen, he could find their payroll information and understand that. Then there were the expenses. Okay, that part made sense. But then this little section with more expenses down here? What was up with that? There were little buttons with abbreviations in them to select throughout the page, but no matter how much he looked around, he couldn't find a help guide in the program to help him to decode what these buttons meant.

The front door unlocked, then opened, and he heard Amelia's footsteps as she walked inside. "Good morning!" she called up to him as she kicked off her shoes.

"Morning!"

Amelia was James's second in command. She was a few years younger than him and ridiculously competent in the field. She walked up the small set of stairs, face a little flushed from the heat and her long, blonde hair pulled up in a messy bun on top of her head.

"Is the air conditioner on?" she called as she got to the top of the short staircase that led into the open kitchen and living room. "It's almost as hot in here as it is outside."

James stood up and picked up his coffee, grateful to look away from the screen for a few minutes. Amelia walked in, wearing shorts and a light tee-shirt and holding her own iced coffee. She raised an eyebrow as she looked at him, and he knew exactly how bad he looked before she even spoke.

"Did you sleep at all?"

"Yeah."

She rolled her eyes and gave him a grim smile. Amelia got it. At least he had that. They might bicker nonstop, but the team at North Worcester County was solid. The others were being as understanding as they could be as James tried to settle into the job.

"I'm fine, I'll sleep more after work," he continued. "I'm just trying to get some of this admin work done before everyone else gets here."

"Is there anything I can help with?"

"Honestly, I'm not sure," James admitted. "Do you know anything about approving the budget?"

Amelia shook her head. "Not at all," she said. "I submitted a gas reimbursement form last week. Is that what it is?"

Crap, he'd forgotten about that. They'd sent it to the Foundation's accounts team and he'd meant to follow up a few days ago. James made a mental note to check on that next. "No, it's like, the entire thing," he said. "I understand payroll and that's about it. There's all these abbreviations and I have no clue what they are."

"And I take it they haven't sent the training information with all of those things."

"Of course not. I feel like a fucking third-grader trying to do this job."

He stretched and his back popped. "I'll figure it out," he said, cracking his neck, then taking a sip of coffee.

Amelia made a face. "You sound like a rice crispy."

"It's what happens when you pass thirty."

That and didn't work out regularly, didn't get enough sleep, and drank coffee for at least one meal a day. He'd get back on it, though. He just needed to catch up on everything and then he could take care of himself again.

"Go take a run," Amelia suggested. "Get some blood flowing. I'll get stuff set up for the meeting and take a look at the air conditioner. If it's just the filters, we might be in luck."

Yes, the meeting he'd forgotten about. The Foundation had sent information for him to share with the team, but it was encrypted. He really did want to take that run though, and since he apparently couldn't get into the information until Bradley got here to help, he might as well do it now.

As James walked toward the stairway at the front of the raised ranch house the Foundation had purchased as their North County headquarters, he cast a longing look down the dim hall toward the three bedrooms they had for overnight staff. But if he fell asleep now, he'd sleep through the meeting. Caffeine and a workout would wake him up enough to function today.

James didn't believe it even as he thought it, but he headed down-stairs anyway.

The first small flight of blue carpeted stairs ended at the front entrance. Through the frosted glass window in the middle of the door, he could see it was overcast outside and he had a vague hope that some rain might break the heat.

He turned and walked down the second flight of stairs, which led to the basement. To the left of the stairs was the closed-up medical room that had been unused since the Foundation eliminated team medics five years before James had joined. He thought briefly about how he should really go in and check the condition of pretty much everything in there, then turned and headed toward the little gym behind the heavy door to the right.

The gym was slightly cooler, one of the benefits of it being in the basement. As the door slammed shut behind him, James went over to the fan in the corner and turned it on, noting the amount of dust that flew off it as the blades began to spin.

This place was getting a little grimy. Not that James was a great housekeeper or expected anyone on the team to do the cleaning in-stead, but the puff of dust made him feel itchy just looking at it. He turned the fan off and unlatched the plastic front casing. There was a clean towel sitting on the shelf next to him, so James gave the fan a quick wipe, then put it back together and turned it on again. It wasn't great, but it was better than nothing.

James went for his workout bag, then realized he'd left it upstairs. For a second, he was about to go back up and get it. But if he did that, then he'd end up thinking of something else that needed to be done. He'd go do that, then there'd be no time to do his workout. And then he'd have to listen to Amelia lecture him about not getting any exercise.

Nothing in the bag was necessary. His headphones were upstairs, but Amelia had left her speaker down here. So James hooked it up to his phone, turned on his usual workout playlist, and started stretching. If he could lose himself in his workout for a little while, it would be a step in the right direction. Then hopefully the day would go smoothly and he could try to settle into this new role a little better.

ABOUT THE AUTHOR

AMANDA MCCORMACK IS THE author of *North County Paranormal Unit*, the *New Winslow* series, and the urban fantasy novella *The Problem with Magic*. She's a lifelong Massachusetts resident whose passion for the region provides the inspiration behind a lot of her work. She loves ghost stories, public transit, and buying more candles than she'll ever actually use.

Contact Amanda at amanda (at) enfieldarts.com

ALSO BY AMANDA MCCORMACK

Jarvis Street: North County Paranormal #2

JAMES NEVER WANTED TO be in charge.

Never wanted to move up in the Foundation.

But heavy is the head that wears the crown and all that, right?

It's been one month since James was assigned the captaincy at the North County Branch of the Foundation for Paranormal Studies. He's exhausted, undertrained, and buried under mountains of paperwork when he'd rather be out in the field doing what he does best.

As new requirements come through for branch teams, North County is handed a fresh case to solve. The Jarvis Street School is long abandoned and about to be converted into condos. But before any construction can be done, the violent spirits haunting the building need to be removed.

What starts as a simple case becomes more complicated, with the team fiercely debating their moral responsibilities as new details come to light. Add in some simmering resentments, glitchy equipment, and what might or might not be the ghost of their murderous former captain following James around. Will James be able to keep his team together through this first real test of his leadership skills?

Jarvis Street is Book 2 in the North County Paranormal Unit Series, a paranormal workplace urban fantasy!

***

New Winslow

"You know, people don't exactly need a reason to stay in New Winslow."

A small town in the grip of a mysterious curse.
A population trying to live in its shadow.
And an impulsive promise that brings home two friends years after they left for good.

In New Winslow, stories weave in and out of each other. The town psychic seeks answers to something bigger than herself. Four friends warily reunite. And a man has made the most of his life, despite being trapped here for decades.

All that's been buried is slowly resurfacing. But will it change anything in a town that refuses to acknowledge its curse?

Find New Winslow on your favorite online retailer!

www.ingramcontent.com/pod-product-compliance
Lightning Source LLC
Chambersburg PA
CBHW021441150726
47989CB00001B/342